MW01136175

Sonrise Stable
Outward Appearances

Vicki Watson

Illustrated by Becky Raber
& Janet Griffin-Scott

Copyright © 2013 by Vicki Watson

Sonrise Stable: Outward Appearances by Vicki Watson

Printed in the United States of America

ISBN 978-0-9847242-4-6

All rights reserved solely by the author. The author guarantees all contents are original and do not infringe upon the legal rights of any other person or work. No part of this book may be reproduced in any form without the permission of the author.

Scripture taken from the New King James Version®. Copyright © 1982 by Thomas Nelson, Inc. Used by permission.

Illustrated by Becky Raber

Cover and chapter 4 illustration by Janet Griffin-Scott

But the Lord said to Samuel, "Do not look at his appearance or at his physical stature, because I have refused him. For the Lord does not see as man sees; for man looks at the outward appearance, but the Lord looks at the heart.

1 Samuel 16:7

Sonrise Stable Characters *(Horses in Parentheses)*

Grandma *(Kezzie)*

Lisa and Robert	Kristy and Eric	Julie *(Elektra)* and Jonathan
Lauren	Rosie *(Scamper)*	Jared *(Scout)*
	Carrie *(Bandit)*	Jessie *(Patches)*
	(co-own Majestic)	Jamie *(Pearl)*

Billy: Eighteen-year-old employee of Sonrise Stable *(Sassy)*

Jeremy - son of nurse mare farm owner where Majestic was born

Cats: June Bug, Katy, Jemimah, Cowboy, Sparrow

Dog: Tick

Sonrise Stable

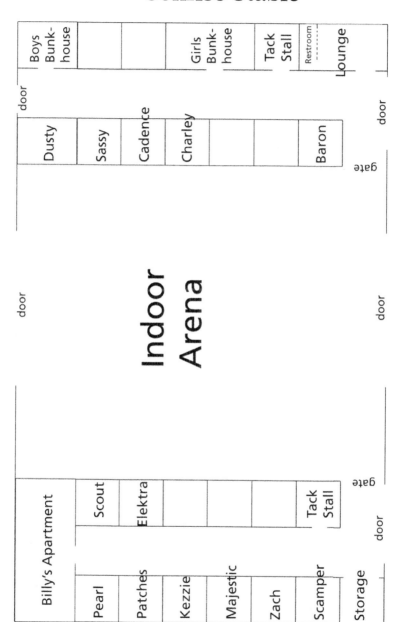

Chapter 1

Majestic's Homecoming

Rosie beamed with pride as she led her brown-and-white foal out of the back of the trailer. Majestic stepped down onto the driveway, his tiny hooves crunching the gravel. He whinnied and raised his head, surveying his new home.

The horses in the barn returned the greeting, welcoming the newest arrival to Sonrise Stable. The twins joined Rosie and Carrie around the foal.

"Aw, he's beautiful!" Jamie squealed. "I want one."

Jessie ran her hand over the foal's coat. "He's so soft!"

The colt was surrounded by girls, but he paid little attention to them. His ears were pricked forward; his large brown eyes focused on the stable. Perhaps memories of his mother stirred within him, and he hoped she might be one of the horses on the other side of the barn door.

"He's so small," Jessie said.

"He's only two weeks old." Rosie patted Majestic's neck. "Carrie and I taught him to drink milk out of a bucket."

Carrie nodded. "Majestic was the cutest and smartest of all the foals at the Last Chance Corral."

Rosie kissed the foal's nose. "It was so much fun, but I'm glad to be home. I can't wait to see Scamper."

Jessie crossed her arms and frowned. "I don't know why Jamie and I couldn't go to Last Chance. Why do you guys get to have all the fun?"

"You're pretty young for something like that," Rosie said. "Maybe when you're a little old—"

Jessie's face turned so red it appeared steam would start billowing out her ears. Before Rosie could get out of the way, Jessie lowered her head and butted her in the stomach.

"Ooomph!" Rosie fell to the ground and groaned in pain.

Grandma stepped around from the front of the trailer. "What's going—"

A horrible screeching sound caused them all to look toward the barn.

"Sassy! No!" A deep voice yelled.

Rosie rolled over, clasping her hands over her ears. The barn door bulged outward so far she was certain it was going to break in half. There was a crash, a clatter of hooves, and a large dark-brown mule popped through the mangled door.

Sassy paused for a moment looking a little stunned. She shook her head, her long ears flopping back and forth, then she spotted the foal and took off toward him at a high-speed trot.

Rosie's eyes widened. "Oh, no!" Sassy was running straight at her. She slipped on the gravel, but finally gained enough traction to scramble to her feet. Carrie and the twins bolted for cover behind the trailer as the thundering mule drew closer.

Billy ran out of the barn holding Sassy's halter in one hand and the lead rope in the other. His face was beet-red. "Sassy! Whoa! Come back here, you old—"

Sassy didn't even slow down. She was focused like a laser on the colt.

Grandma grabbed the lead rope from Rosie and shoved her in the direction of the other girls. Sassy slid to a stop inches from the foal. Majestic stared up at the massive creature towering over him. With her large head and huge ears, the mule bore almost no resemblance to his mother, but he didn't appear to be afraid.

Sassy lowered her head and touched noses with the colt. She sniffed him all over and began making strange little grunting sounds.

Billy slapped his leg with the end of the lead rope and glared at Sassy. "That dad-burned mule! She about trampled me."

Rosie left her hideout behind the horse trailer, trying to brush off the seat of her pants which was uncomfortably wet from where she had fallen on the driveway. She cocked her head sideways and stared at the mule. "What is she doing?"

"She seems to think Majestic is her baby." Grandma turned to Billy. "What exactly were you doing with her?"

Billy frowned and rubbed the back of his neck. "I was planning to take her over to the other side of the barn to free up her stall for the foal, but as soon as I opened her door, that little guy—" he pointed at Majestic, "squealed. Sassy apparently thought he was calling her. She barreled out of the stall and would have run right over me if I hadn't jumped out of the way. Then she stuck her head through the crack in the door and pushed until it popped open."

Billy leaned over and tried to slip the halter over the mule's head.

Grandma waved her hand. "No need for that. She's not going anywhere. I don't think a stick of dynamite could get her away from this foal."

Rosie spun around to face her grandmother. "You're not going to let Sassy be his mother, are you?"

"No," Grandma laughed. "We can certainly find a better role model for him than this mule."

Kristy came out of the other side of the barn and joined the group, along with Julie and her son, Jared.

"Why did you bring Sassy out here, Billy? We were waiting for you to bring her over to her new stall." Julie bent down to pet Majestic. "You are every bit as cute as Rosie said."

"I didn't exactly *bring* her out." Billy pointed to the damaged door at the left side of the barn.

"Oh no! Eric won't be happy when he sees that," Kristy said.

Jared elbowed Billy. "I thought you were the mule whisperer."

"I'm the mule whisperer all right. I have a few things I'm going to whisper in this mule's ear as soon as I get her back in a stall." Billy gave Sassy an extra hard "pat" on her rump, but she was so busy examining her baby she didn't seem to notice.

Grandma handed Majestic's lead back to Rosie. "Take him inside. I don't think we'll get this mule to budge any other way."

Rosie walked toward the barn with the colt following close beside her. Sassy stuck to him like glue on the opposite side.

Julie pointed out Sassy's stall near the end of the aisle. "Take the foal in there. Circle around quickly and come back out."

Rosie led the foal in, with Sassy right at his heels. Billy stood ready at the stall door. As soon as Rosie and the colt were out, he slammed the door shut. Before she knew what had happened, Sassy found herself alone in the stall. She circled the small area, frantically butting her head against the door to see if she could get it to pop open like the other door had.

Grandma frowned at Billy. "You need to teach your mule some manners."

"My mule?" He looked at her. "What do you mean? She's your mule."

"I think it's time to officially transfer ownership to you. You've done so well with her, and Kezzie's leg has healed enough for me to ride her again."

Rosie watched a smile spread across Billy's face. She shook her head, amazed that anyone would be excited about owning that animal. Apparently Billy was.

He hung Sassy's halter and lead rope on the front of the stall and turned back to Grandma. "You really mean it? She's mine?"

Grandma smiled and patted him on the shoulder. "Yes. She's all yours."

Billy leaned forward against the stall, looking in at the mule who was still trying to figure out where her foal had gone. "Did you hear that, Sassy? You're mine now."

"I'm too old to deal with a strong-willed mule," Grandma said. "I think you'll both learn a lot from each other."

Rosie turned the foal around to take him to his stall on the other side of the barn. "I bet Cadence is anxious to get out of the trailer."

"Oh dear! With all the excitement I totally forgot about her." Grandma hurried down the aisle.

"You can put her next to Sassy," Billy suggested as the group headed outside. "Maybe having a new friend will distract her from the foal."

"Good idea," Rosie agreed. She hoped Sassy would become best friends with the new mare and forget all about Majestic.

"Sassy might have another friend soon," Kristy announced.

Rosie looked over Majestic's neck at her mother. "Who?"

"While you were at Last Chance, we had several people stop here to ask about boarding. A Mr. Taylor is bringing his daughter's horse tomorrow."

Rosie stopped Majestic. "Our first boarder? That's great!" She couldn't wait until they were making enough money to allow her mom and dad to quit their jobs. Then everyone would work together at the stable. She and Carrie were already doing their part by feeding the horses and cleaning stalls.

Jessie tugged at Grandma's sleeve. "Can Jamie and I go to Last Chance Corral next year and get our own foal? It's not fair that Rosie and Carrie got to go and we had to stay home."

Grandma put her arm around Jessie. "You show me that you're mature enough, and I'll think about it." She nodded toward Rosie. "Knocking your cousin over wasn't a good start."

Rosie felt a twinge of guilt. She shouldn't have teased Jessie about being too young. After all, the twins were only two years younger than her and Carrie, and both had been riding for longer than either of them. "Jessie, you can help us get Majestic settled in his stall, and then we'll show you Sparrow."

"Sparrow? Is that another foal?" Jessie asked.

"No, not quite," Rosie laughed. "Wait until you hear Sparrow's story." She offered Jessie the lead rope. "Do you want to lead him?"

Jessie smiled and took the rope. "Sorry for knocking you down."

"It's okay."

The girls started down the aisle; the colt content to follow them wherever they went.

Chapter 2

Katrina and Baron

Rosie paused as she neared Majestic's stall. She set the bucket of milk down in the aisle and listened to Carrie.

"You're kind of sad aren't you? I know how you feel. I lost my mother too."

She looked through the partially open door, watching her sister talk to the foal. She studied her face, but couldn't read her feelings.

Carrie leaned back against the wall, put her hand under Majestic's chin, and kissed his muzzle. "Don't worry. You'll like it at Sonrise Stable." The colt's brown eyes locked onto hers, and she stroked his neck.

Katy and Jemimah had followed Rosie and were trying to drink the foal's milk. "No, girls. I already fed you. Go catch a mouse or something." She shooed the cats away and picked up the bucket.

Rosie entered the stall and slipped the handle of the bucket into a snap hanging from a ring on the wall. The girls stood side by side watching the hungry foal drink.

Rosie laughed at the slurping sounds Majestic made as he eagerly consumed his breakfast. She combed through his short, soft mane with her fingers and grew more serious. "Are you okay, Carrie? You look sad."

"I'm okay." Carrie lifted her eyes from the foal and turned toward Rosie. "I've been thinking about how Majestic and the other foals were taken away from their mothers so suddenly, and it started me thinking about my parents."

Rosie felt her heart make a strange little thump. She didn't like it when Carrie talked about her biological parents. "But my parents are your parents now. They're our parents." She stared at her sister. "Aren't you happy here?"

"Of course. I love Mom and Dad and Grandma—everyone." Carrie ran her hand down the colt's back and walked around him so she was standing on the opposite side, facing Rosie. "Usually I don't even think about my other parents, but sometimes I just feel different."

"What do you mean?"

"Well …," Carrie hesitated. "For one thing, I don't look like any of you. You all have dark hair and brown eyes—and look at me." Carrie flipped her hair over her shoulder. "I'm all pale with blonde hair and blue eyes."

Rosie grinned the silly grin that meant she had a crazy idea.

Carrie looked at her. "What?"

"I could dye my hair blonde."

"Can you imagine the look on Grandma's face if you waltzed in with blonde hair?"

They both laughed so loudly that the foal stopped drinking. He turned his head to look at Carrie, then looked over at Rosie. Milk trickled down his muzzle. He wiggled his upper lip as if he were trying to laugh with them. That made the girls laugh even more.

Billy peeked into the stall. "What's so hilarious?"

Rosie was laughing so hard her stomach ached. She gasped for air. "I'm going to—" She looked at Carrie and then burst into another fit of laughter.

Billy shook his head. "Girls! I'll never understand them." He patted the colt. "You and I need to stick together, buddy."

He turned back to the girls. "Grab your hammers and meet me on the other side of the barn. Your dad wants you two to help me with the girls' bunkhouse today."

Rosie saluted Billy as he left. She sucked in a deep breath, held it a while, then slowly let it out. "You're a Jackson now, Carrie. It doesn't matter what color your hair is."

"I guess not," Carrie said.

"But if you ever want me to—"

"No!" Carrie waved her hands. "Don't even start that again. Let's go build a bunkhouse!"

The girls each gave Majestic a hug, gently pushing him back when he tried to follow them out of the stall. He whinnied as they closed the door.

"Aw." Rosie stopped and put her hand over her heart. "Doesn't it hurt you right here when he does that?"

Carrie nodded. "I wish we could stay with him all the time so he wouldn't be lonely."

"Yeah, me too, but Grandma says that wouldn't be good for him. He needs to be around other horses so they can teach him how to be a horse. Scamper had to learn the same thing when he was little."

The girls walked across the arena to the other side of the barn. Rosie stopped at the buckskin mare's stall and stroked her forehead. "Cadence, what do you think of your new neighbor?"

Sassy pushed her nose against the metal bars that separated their stalls and sniffed at the mare. Cadence squealed and tossed her head.

Carrie giggled and pointed to a cardboard sign tacked onto the stall. "Sassy—Owned by William King."

"William King?" Rosie laughed. "Who's that?"

Billy dropped a stack of boards in the aisle and headed their direction. "What are you laughing at? It's my new image. After all, I own my own mule now."

"I can't imagine calling you William," Carrie said.

"You'll always be Billy to us." Rosie was still surprised by how excited he was about owning Sassy. Billy had been riding her since last fall when he came to help remodel the run-down farmhouse. No one else was able to get the mule to do much of anything, even her Aunt Julie who was a horse trainer.

Rosie looked around at the stack of wood on the floor, trying to imagine how Billy was going to turn two horse stalls into a bunkhouse. She held up her hammer. "I'm ready. Where do we start?"

Billy looked skeptical. "Let me see what you two can do." He handed each of the girls a scrap piece of two by four. "How about a contest? Let's see which of you can drive a nail all the way into one of these boards first."

Rosie looked over at Carrie, and her sister nodded.

"Okay," Billy said. "On your mark—"

Rosie dropped down to her knees and positioned the nail between the thumb and first finger of her left hand. She gripped the hammer with her right.

"Get set— Go!"

Rosie tapped the nail a couple times, then totally missed it the next few times, putting several dents in the board. She glanced over at Carrie who had stopped altogether, shaking the finger she had apparently just pounded. Rosie gave an extra hard swing, and the nail flipped out of her fingers and across the stall.

"Whoa!" Billy made a time-out sign with his hands. "You both hammer like girls."

Rosie looked at Carrie and laughed. "We are girls, Billy."

Billy held his hand out. "Let me see your hammer."

Rosie gave it to him. He flipped the hammer up in the air and caught it with one hand. "Where did you get this thing?"

"I bought it." Rosie snatched the hammer back. "I liked it because it was red."

Billy rolled his eyes. "Leave it to a girl to buy a tool based on what it looks like." He pulled out his battered black-and-gray hammer that looked as if it had been through a war. With three strokes he hammered a nail all the way into one of the scrap boards.

"With that light thing—" Billy pointed to Rosie's hammer, "you have to do all the work." He held up his own hammer. "If the weight is properly balanced, you just swing, and the tool does the work."

"Let me try." Rosie took Billy's hammer and jabbed at the nail a few times.

"No." Billy shook his head. "Don't poke at it. Swing it."

Rosie took a longer stroke and hit the nail solidly for the first time. "Oh, wow! That was a lot easier."

Billy smiled. "Now you're getting it."

"Here, Carrie, you—" Rosie stopped in mid sentence, as she looked down the aisle and saw a trailer coming down the drive. "The boarder is here!" She dropped the hammer and both girls sprinted toward the door. A black truck backed a shiny silver horse trailer up to the barn.

Grandma stepped out of the house. Tick shot past her and ran toward the stable, barking at the newcomers. Rosie grabbed a lead rope and clipped it to the dog's collar. "Shh, Tick, you're going to scare our first customer away."

The Rottweiler sat down between the girls and licked Rosie's hand. "Yech." She wiped the dog slobber off on her jeans. When the truck stopped, a tall blonde girl who looked to be about fourteen, stepped out of the passenger side. A man remained in the truck, talking on a cell phone.

"Hello." Grandma extended her hand. "You must be Katrina Taylor. Welcome to Sonrise Stable. These are my granddaughters, Rosie and Carrie."

Katrina shook Grandma's hand and nodded at the girls.

Rosie's eyes were drawn like a magnet to the girl's face. A silver ring looped through one nostril. Each ear had multiple piercings, and Rosie could see a tattoo of some sort on her arm, partially hidden by Katrina's left sleeve. She couldn't help rubbing her own nose, imagining how painful it must be to poke a hole through it. She noticed Carrie staring at the girl too.

"Dad. I need your help," Katrina called impatiently.

Her father finished his conversation and tossed his phone onto the truck seat. He stretched and looked around. The crab apple trees were in full bloom, and the grass that had been a drab brown all winter was almost entirely green now. "Isn't this great? I think Baron's going to like it here."

"More than I will, that's for sure." Katrina crossed her arms hugging them tightly to her thin body. "Why did we have to move to Ohio, Dad? It's freezing."

"This is pretty warm for April. Wait until you see what January is like." Rosie pushed on Tick's hindquarters, trying to make her sit. The dog was doing her best to break free so she could greet the guests. "Sit still," Rosie scolded.

Katrina rolled her eyes and muttered, "I'd better not be here in January."

Rosie shifted her attention away from the dog and back to Katrina. "I'm sorry, what did you say?"

The girl shook her head. "Nothing."

Carrie walked over to help Rosie with the dog. "Where are you from, Katrina?"

"Florida. It's never cold there." She opened the side door and snapped a lead rope onto her horse's halter. When she nodded, her father lowered the ramp at the back. A tall dark bay gelding backed out.

"He's beautiful," Carrie said.

Rosie looked the horse over. "Is he a Quarter Horse?"

Katrina turned up her nose and sniffed. "Baron is an off-the-track Thoroughbred. I'm training him for dressage." She started toward the barn. "Which stall is his?"

Rosie motioned to her. "Follow me. You're our first boarder so you can pick any stall you want."

15

Rosie led the way down the aisle. "This is Cadence. She's a Tennessee Walking Horse, and this—"

Sassy interrupted her with a prolonged greeting to Baron. Her peculiar voice sounded like a cross between a horse's neigh and a donkey's bray.

Everyone laughed—except Katrina. She backed Baron away from Sassy's stall. "I really don't want my horse near that—that thing—whatever it is!"

Rosie glanced at Billy, who had just joined them. She saw a flash of anger in his eyes.

"That *thing* happens to be a mule. Her name is Sassy, and she belongs to me."

Katrina glared at him in silence, then turned Baron around and led him back toward the front of the barn.

"We're turning these two stalls into a bunkhouse for our summer camps," Grandma explained hastily, "but here—" She pointed to the first stall on the left side of the aisle. "How about this one? You'll be right across from the lounge and close to the tack stall."

Katrina led Baron inside and removed his halter. She turned coolly to Billy. "I suppose you'll be feeding him and cleaning his stall?"

"Uh, no. That's their job." Billy pointed with both index fingers toward Rosie and Carrie.

"Oh." Katrina looked them over as if she thought they were too young to take care of her horse. "He's used to being fed promptly at 6 a.m. and 6 p.m.—only the best hay and grain for my boy." She patted Baron's shoulder.

Grandma frowned. "We'll take good care of Baron, but he'll have to be on the same schedule as the other horses. They get upset if another horse is fed and they're not."

Katrina didn't look pleased. She turned back to the girls. "He hates having a messy stall, so you should clean it two or three times a day."

Rosie raised her eyebrows and looked at Carrie.

"Don't forget to turn him out at least once every day for exercise. And double, no triple check that his stall door is always latched. If not, he'll get it open. He's very smart." Katrina turned to her dad "What about a blanket? He might get cold tonight."

"He'll be fine, honey." Mr. Taylor put his arm on his daughter's shoulder. "He's a horse. You worry too much about him. Come on, let's get your saddle and whatever all that other stuff is you have in the truck."

Rosie tugged Carrie's arm. "Come on. Let's get Baron some hay."

As soon as they were out of earshot of the others, Carrie whispered, "Do you think all the boarders will be like her?"

"I sure hope not. I had to leave before she asked if we could put a TV in Baron's stall so he wouldn't get bored."

Carrie laughed. "Grandma would never allow that. You know how she hates TV."

Rosie stepped onto the first rung of the ladder to the loft. "Whew! Having a riding stable is not going to be as easy as I thought."

.

Chapter 3

Outward Appearances

Rosie grabbed a pen and the County Classifieds and leaped onto the brown leather couch beside Carrie. They had just finished lunch after returning home from church. Sparrow climbed up between the two girls.

Carrie wagged her finger at the cat. "Listen, little girl, you're supposed to take it easy after your surgery. No climbing allowed." The plain-looking brown tiger cat made a chirping sound and flopped over on her left side, stretching out along Carrie's leg.

Rosie leaned down to look at Sparrow's wound and cringed. "I sure wish they could find the person who shot her."

Grandma made herself comfortable in the easy chair across from the girls and set her cup of coffee on the end table. "I'm afraid there's not much chance of that now. A cat shot with an arrow won't be a high priority for the police department."

"It's not fair." Rosie remembered the night she and Carrie had found Sparrow at Last Chance—with the arrow still sticking through her. She shook her head, trying to erase the awful picture from her mind. "Where did Mom and Dad go?"

"Your dad and Billy went out to fix the barn door Sassy damaged," Grandma said.

Rosie jumped up and walked over to the window. "Mom's out there too. Oh, no. It looks like it's going to rain again. We're never going to be able to ride on our trails!"

She returned to the couch and picked up the newspaper, thumbing through the pages.

Carrie leaned toward her sister. "What are you planning to buy?"

"Horses for our summer camp." Rosie grinned. "How many do we need?"

Carrie began counting off horses on her fingers—Kezzie, Scamper, Zach, Sassy, Scout, Patches, Pearl, Elektra. We have eight now if we use all our horses."

"Hmm," Rosie said. "Aren't you forgetting someone?"

Carrie bumped her forehead with the palm of her hand. "Oh, Cadence. I forgot all about her. Make that nine."

"We'll start off small this year," Grandma explained, "taking about ten campers at a time on the trail rides."

"And Carrie and I can be trail guides," Rosie said.

Grandma nodded. "I think three guides per ride will work—one in the front and two in the back."

Rosie did some quick calculations. "That makes thirteen horses all together—so we need four more." She flipped through several pages until she located the livestock section and scanned the ads. "Ah, here's one." She read out loud, "Six-year-old Standardbred-Paint gelding, bought as a three-year-old, Amish said he was broke to ride and drive, we only rode him a few times, needs more saddle time, $500 OBO."

"Oh-Bo?" Carrie repeated. "What's that?"

"O-B-O," Grandma said each letter. "It stands for 'or best offer.' It means they'll take less than the price listed in the ad."

"Why do they put a price in there at all if they're telling people they will take less than that?" Carrie asked. "That doesn't make sense."

"I guess it gives everyone a starting point to bargain from," Grandma said. "I've done quite a bit of horse trading in my time and can usually get a horse for a lot less than they're advertised for."

Rosie looked up at her grandmother. "What do you think about that one?"

"Keep looking. I've never heard of a Standardbred-Paint cross. Anyway that horse is way too green to be used with our campers."

"Green?" Rosie glanced at the ad again. "Actually, it doesn't say what color he is."

Grandma shook her head and looked at Carrie. "I guess Rosie thinks if she can't be successful as an artist, she'll become a comedian."

Carrie grinned. "But don't you have to be funny to be a comedian?"

"Hey." Rosie swatted her on the head with the newspaper. "At least I'm funnier than you are!"

Carrie put her hand out to protect Sparrow. "Look out. You're scaring the cat." Sparrow stared at Rosie with her eyes all bugged out.

Rosie scanned the paper again. "Okay, here's another one—12-year-old black mare, Forbidden, beautiful horse, tons of spunk, needs experienced rider …" Rosie stopped

21

midway through the ad and shook her head. "Uh, yeah, never mind about that one."

"You have to be careful buying horses," Grandma warned. "Unfortunately people aren't always honest when they want to sell one. For our camps we need safe, well-trained horses."

Rosie turned the page. "Oh! Here we go. This one sounds cute! Eight-year-old red roan Quarter Horse mare, Tilly is 14 hands and is a gorgeous red roan, great personality $1500."

Rosie looked over the top of the paper. "Can we go look at her? I love red roans."

"We have a lot of different colored horses, but we don't have any roans," Carrie said. "Let's see. Zach's a palomino. Kezzie is chestnut. Cadence is buckskin."

"Sassy's brown. Scamper is black-and-white, and Majestic is brown-and-white," Rosie said.

"Elektra is bay," Carrie added.

Rosie nodded. "A red roan would be perfect."

Grandma took a sip of coffee and stared down into the cup. "First Samuel 16:7."

Rosie and Carrie looked at each other, then turned to their grandmother. "What?"

"For the Lord does not see as man sees; for man looks at the outward appearance, but the Lord looks at the heart."

"O-kay," Rosie said slowly, not seeing her grandmother's point.

"It's like your hammer," Carrie said eagerly. "Don't you get it?"

"Well." Rosie tried to think. "They're both red."

"Remember? Billy said you shouldn't buy a hammer because of what it looks like."

"Yeah, I know that." Rosie found it a little annoying when Carrie picked up things faster than she did. After all she was the older sister by two months. She set the paper on her lap and leaned back on the couch, waiting for the explanation she knew would be coming.

Grandma set her coffee down and walked across the living room. Rosie sometimes wondered if her grandmother would be able to talk if she wasn't allowed to walk or use her hands.

"Because Saul disobeyed, God rejected him as king over Israel. God then sent Samuel to a man named Jesse to pick the new king. Seven of Jesse's sons came before Samuel, each strong and handsome, but God said no to all of them."

Grandma stopped and turned to the girls. "Samuel was confused, because God had told him the next king would be one of Jesse's sons. Then he learned that there was one more son in the field tending the sheep. When that son appeared, God told Samuel that this one, although he was the youngest, would be the next king. That was King—?" Grandma paused, testing the girls to see whether they knew the answer.

"David!" Rosie shouted in her eagerness to answer before Carrie could.

"That's right." Grandma nodded.

Rosie felt a bit sad. "So I'm not supposed to like red roan horses anymore?"

"No," Grandma laughed. "That's not what I meant. It's just that the ad doesn't say anything about the horse's training or how much and where she's been ridden or if she

23

would be safe for kids. And those things are much more important than what color she is."

Rosie read the ad again. "You're right. It doesn't say much about her."

Grandma looked at the ad over Rosie's shoulder. "But I love red roans too, so I think we should go look at her and see what's in Tilly's heart. Then we can decide whether she would fit in with the rest of the gang at Sonrise Stable."

"Yes!" Rosie drew a big circle around the ad, ripped the page out, and handed it to her grandmother.

Grandma folded the paper and set it on the coffee table. "Have you ever heard the saying, 'A good horse is never a bad color?'"

The girls shook their heads.

"It's always struck me as the horseman's version of 1 Samuel 16:7. When you have a really good horse, you don't care what color it is. You don't even think about it."

"Oh! Oh!" Rosie jumped off the couch, startling the cat again. "Oops, sorry girl." She turned and patted Sparrow's head.

Carrie gently pulled the cat up onto her lap to protect her. "What crazy idea do you have now?"

"Grandma just gave me an inspiration for another T-shirt design! I can draw a bunch of horses of all different colors and put that saying—'A good horse is never a bad color'—underneath it."

Rosie dashed upstairs and returned a few minutes later with her sketch pad and pencil. She sat down beside Carrie and began drawing.

Grandma walked over to the window. "The door looks a lot better already. That's good; our second boarder will be here tomorrow. I don't want to make a bad first impression."

Rosie looked up from her sketch pad. "I hope whoever it is isn't as bossy as Katrina." *Oops!* As soon as the words were out of her mouth, she realized it wasn't a nice thing to say. She looked at her grandmother to see whether she was angry at her.

"Let's give Katrina a chance. Maybe she was worried about whether we would take good care of Baron."

"Why do people get all those piercings like she has?" Carrie asked.

"She has a tattoo on her arm too," Rosie added.

"Oh?" Grandma's eyebrows went up. "I didn't notice that."

"Part of it was covered by her sleeve. I couldn't tell what it was." Rosie shaded in the first horse's mane. "I think tattoos are creepy-looking."

She could sense her grandmother staring at her. She needed to be more careful about saying everything that popped into her head. Were tattoos a 1 Samuel 16:7 thing too? She began sketching the next horse in the design.

Chapter 4

Hannah and Dusty

Carrie dumped a scoop of grain into the feeder, and Rosie stuffed two flakes of hay into Baron's rack. The horses were more hungry than usual that morning since the girls had been late getting to the barn.

The twins were playing fetch with Tick and Cowboy in the barn aisle. The cat was a better retriever than the dog. He loved to chase the stuffed mouse the girls threw for him.

"Are you done feeding now?" Jessie asked.

Rosie nodded and picked a few pieces of hay out of her hair.

"Great!" Jamie smiled. "You and Carrie can ride with us."

Rosie leaned down to pat Tick and pulled the nylon dog bone out of her mouth. She tossed it down the aisle, and the Rottweiler took off after it, nearly knocking poor Cowboy over. "We still have stalls to clean, and the new boarder should be here any minute."

"If you two helped, we'd get done faster," Carrie said.

Jessie groaned and selected a purple pitchfork hanging on the wall. "How come every time I come over here, you make me work?"

Billy whistled as he walked by the girls carrying a sheet of plywood. "Work is good for you. When you all are done cleaning stalls, you can help me."

"Nah." Jessie shook her head. "Since you like work so much, we wouldn't want to deprive you of your joy. Besides, Jared's coming over in a while to help you."

"Come on," Rosie said. "We're never going to get to ride if we don't get busy. Carrie and I will clean Baron's stall. You and Jamie can do Cadence's. Just stay away from that crazy mule."

Billy poked his head out of the bunkhouse stall. "I heard that. Stop picking on my mule."

"I'm not picking on old Mulehead, just telling the truth. She is crazy. I've never seen Scamper try to run through a door. He's too smart to—"

"Yeah, yeah, whatever." Billy squeezed the trigger on his saw, drowning out the sound of Rosie's voice and sending the barn cats scrambling for safety.

Although Rosie had forgiven Billy for the incident at the horse show the year before and now viewed him as sort of an older brother, he still annoyed her at times. "Your mule is crazy," she shouted. She could barely hear herself above the noise of the saw, so she gave up and went back to work. Just as she and Carrie finished Baron's stall, Katrina walked into the barn. "Oh, no," Rosie mumbled.

Katrina pulled out her cell phone and glanced at it. "You just fed him? It's 9:30!"

Rosie looked down and kicked at a small stone on the floor. "Mom and Grandma left early this morning, and Carrie and I overslept."

"Sorry," Carrie said. "Usually we have everyone fed by 8:30."

Katrina stuffed the phone into her pocket and flung both arms out to her sides. "Now what am I going to do? I finally have a day off of school, and now I have to sit around here and wait for my horse to finish eating before I can ride—all because you were too lazy to get out of bed!"

There was an awkward silence. Rosie considered asking Katrina to help them clean the rest of the stalls, but quickly realized that wasn't a good idea.

The twins came out of Cadence's stall and headed their direction. *Oh, no.* Rosie tried to get Jessie's attention to signal her to keep quiet, but her cousin was staring intently at Katrina.

"Rosie said you have a tattoo on your arm. Can I see it?"

Katrina frowned at her, then pulled the sleeve of her sweatshirt back to reveal the word "Chase" tattooed on her forearm.

Jessie moved closer to her. "Eww. Why'd you get that? My mom says only sailors are supposed to have tattoos."

Rosie cringed, expecting Katrina to be angry. She was surprised when the girl laughed.

"You're not allowed to have them until you're eighteen, but a friend of a friend did this one for me. I think it looks cool." Katrina pulled her sleeve back down and turned to watch Baron eat.

"What does it mean?" Jessie persisted. "Do you like to chase people?"

Katrina rolled her eyes. "Don't be ridiculous. Chase is my boyfriend's name."

"Oh." Jessie continued to stare at her. "Doesn't that nose ring hurt?"

And I thought I had a problem with saying whatever popped into my head, Rosie thought. She was about to put her hand over Jessie's mouth and lock her in one of the stalls when Tick started barking. Rosie turned to look out the front door. "That must be the next boarder!"

"Good," Katrina said. "Maybe Baron can have a real horse next to him."

Billy marched down the aisle, brushing sawdust off his jeans. "Excuse me, girls. Your grandmother asked me to take charge if she wasn't back from town in time."

The girls parted to let Billy through. Rosie and the others followed him out the door. This truck and trailer weren't as fancy as Katrina's, but not as bad as Billy's rusty pickup either. A young woman, who looked to be in her early twenties, stepped out of the truck.

Billy held out his hand. "Welcome to Sonrise Stable. I'm William King."

Rosie looked at Carrie and laughed.

"Who's William King?" Jessie said in a loud whisper.

The woman smiled and shook his hand. "I'm Hannah."

Billy peeked through the slats in the side of the trailer. "Who do we have in here?"

"This is Dusty." Hannah snapped the lead onto her horse's halter while Billy opened the trailer door and lowered the ramp.

"It's okay, Dust." Hannah stroked his neck. "Back." The horse backed slowly out. "Good boy." She patted him and let him stand for a minute.

From her position behind the trailer, Rosie looked past the horse's hindquarters and watched Billy close the door. When he turned toward Dusty, he paused briefly and a strange look passed over his face.

Billy hurried past the horse. "Umm, right this way."

Hannah turned Dusty around and started toward the stable. He was an Appaloosa—almost pure white with only a few spots.

"What's wrong with him?" Jessie pointed toward Dusty's head. "Ew! Look at his eyes."

Once again Rosie wanted to put a muzzle on her younger cousin, but she too was staring at the horse's eyes. Dusty's face was white, with mottled pink skin around his eyes and muzzle, typical for an Appaloosa; however, his eyes were sunken and pinkish-red with a small dark rectangle in the center. It made Rosie's eyes hurt to look at them, but she couldn't seem to look away either.

Hannah stopped near the girls. "Oh! I'm sorry. I thought you all knew. Dusty is blind."

"He's blind?" Rosie glanced at Hannah. "What do you do with him?" She held out her hand so Dusty could smell it, then patted his neck. "I mean, I've never been around a blind horse before. You can't ride him, can you?"

Carrie and the twins walked up beside Rosie and patted Dusty, but Katrina stood back and watched.

"I ride him all the time," Hannah said.

"Really?" Rosie couldn't understand how you could ride a blind horse.

The girls followed Hannah and Dusty toward the barn. Katrina caught up with them and spoke quietly. "Just what Baron needs—another freakish animal in the stable."

Rosie turned and glared at her. Grandma had said they needed to give her a chance. She was trying hard to like Katrina, but the girl wasn't making it easy. When Rosie turned back around, she almost tripped over Jamie, who had stepped right in front of her. "What are you doing? Watch where you're going!"

Jamie blinked. "Sorry! I had my eyes closed, trying to imagine what it would be like to be blind."

Jessie immediately closed her eyes, stretched out both arms, and took a few steps. "Ew, I would hate it!"

"Me too!" Carrie said.

"This is Katrina's horse," Billy explained as they walked past Baron's stall. "This is Cadence, one of our lesson horses." He stopped in front of Sassy's stall and turned to face them, a big smile on his face. "And this is my mule, Sassy."

When she spotted Dusty, Sassy launched into her unique mulish welcome. She always seemed hopeful that the next resident of Sonrise Stable would become her best friend. Well, any kind of friend would be a start, since so far none of the animals were overly fond of her.

Hannah laughed. "Aw, I love mules."

Billy looked surprised. "You do?"

"Yeah. I've always wanted one."

Katrina rolled her eyes and shook her head. "Whatever."

"You can ride her sometime if you want," Billy offered.

"Great," Hannah said. "I'd love to. Would the stall on the other side of Sassy be okay for Dusty?"

"Sure. The two end stalls are a little bigger than the others, so he'll have more room." Billy hurried to open the door, and Hannah led Dusty in.

Rosie watched the gelding press his nose against the stall divider and sniff at Sassy. The mule pranced around her stall and squealed at him. Dusty couldn't see her jumbo-sized ears, long head, and thin, ratty tail. He also wouldn't know that Sassy was so fat she looked as if she might foal any day, but maybe none of that was important to horses.

Since he couldn't see any of those things, Rosie wondered how Dusty would decide whether he wanted to be Sassy's friend. And why did Billy like the crazy mule so much? She thought about the Bible verse Grandma had explained to her and Carrie the day before. Could Billy see something in Sassy that she couldn't?

Hannah turned away from Dusty's stall. "While they're getting acquainted, I'll go get my saddle and stuff."

"I can do that for you." Billy latched the stall door and trotted to catch up with Hannah.

"Thank you, William."

Rosie shook her head and watched the two walk down the aisle. She could see Billy chattering away but couldn't hear what he was saying. *Hmm, I don't remember Billy offering to carry Katrina's tack when she arrived.*

Chapter 5

Dusty's Story

"Scoot over, buddy, so I can clean your stall. Why do you have to be such a messy boy?" Rosie patted Scamper's hindquarters. The large black-and-white pony pivoted around and turned to face her. He nuzzled her sleeve, and Rosie hugged him. She hadn't been able to get the blind horse out of her mind as she cleaned stalls the morning after Dusty's arrival. "It's okay. I still love you even if you are messy. I'm so glad you aren't blind. I never thought about horses going blind before."

When the girls finished the stalls, they began getting their horses ready to ride.

Carrie ran a comb through Zach's forelock. The palomino's mane and tail were silky smooth and pure white. "Maybe we should ask Hannah if she wants to ride with us."

Rosie nodded. "That's a good idea."

Jessie peeked out of Patches' stall. "What about Katrina?"

Rosie wasn't thrilled about Katrina riding with them, but she knew it wouldn't be nice to ask Hannah without inviting Katrina also. "I'll go ask them." She ran to the other side of the barn and found Hannah brushing Dusty in his stall.

"We're all going to ride in the arena. Would you like to join us?"

"Sure." Hannah smiled. "Dusty seems to be adjusting well. A short ride would be good for him. We'll be there in a few minutes."

"Great." Rosie looked around. "Have you seen Katrina anywhere?"

"Last time I saw her she was in the lounge."

"Thanks." Rosie headed down the aisle and almost bumped into Billy coming out of the bunkhouse.

"I think I'll get Sassy out and ride too. She could use the exercise."

Rosie thought that was odd. Billy almost never rode with them unless Jared was around, especially when he was in the middle of working on a project. She shrugged. "Sure. Why not?"

As she neared the front of the barn, Rosie could hear Katrina's voice but couldn't see her.

"They brought in this freaky blind horse yesterday. This is like a stable of misfit animals."

Rosie peeked inside Baron's stall. No one there.

"I'm waiting for them to start preaching to me. I think that's why my dad picked this place."

Rosie looked in the lounge. No one there either. She stepped out the front door and saw Katrina sitting on a bench, leaning back against the barn wall.

Katrina jumped up when she saw Rosie. "Hey, gotta go. Talk to you later." She snapped her phone shut and jammed it into the pocket of her jeans. "What are you doing? Spying on me?"

Seriously? Rosie thought. *If I was going to spy on someone, I could certainly do a better job than that.*

"No. I came to ask if you'd like to ride with us in the arena. It's too muddy to go out on the trails. It must have poured down rain last night."

Katrina hesitated. "I don't know."

"Hannah's going to ride with us."

"Oh." Katrina shook her head. "It'll be too crowded. I'll ride when you guys are done." She pulled her phone out again and started texting.

"It's kind of cold out here." Rosie looked at the gray sky and noticed it was starting to drizzle. She nodded toward the door. "You could go in the lounge. It would be drier."

"In a minute. This is the only spot in this crazy place where I can get a signal on my phone." Katrina plopped back down on the bench and continued texting.

Rosie stared at her. "Okay, maybe another time."

Katrina didn't respond.

Rosie shrugged her shoulders and walked back inside. She finished saddling Scamper and led him into the arena where the other girls were already riding. Hannah brought Dusty through the gate on the other side. Billy and Sassy were right behind them.

Rosie mounted Scamper, and he started to move off. She pulled back on the reins. "Whoa, boy. I didn't tell you to go anywhere."

She sat and watched Hannah lead Dusty around the outside of the arena. The other riders gave the two plenty of room. After Hannah walked him around one lap, she mounted and they walked around again.

Rosie cued Scamper to move forward. Soon everyone was riding and joking back and forth as they always did. At times Rosie forgot that Dusty was blind. He seemed just like any of the other horses. Sassy loved him and wanted to be right by his side all the time—or was it more that Billy wanted to be near Hannah? Rosie wasn't sure. She had never seen Billy be so nice to anyone before. Dusty did seem to like Sassy. Maybe the mule had finally found a friend.

After they had ridden a while, Hannah walked Dusty to the middle of the arena and stopped. Everyone brought their horses in and gathered around her.

Rosie couldn't keep herself from staring at the gelding's eyes. It made her own eyes water. She blinked and rubbed them with the back of her hand, then looked at Hannah. "Was Dusty born blind?"

"No. I got him when I was eight. He was three and perfectly healthy. I showed him for years in 4-H—trail, jumping, contesting, parades. You name it, and Dusty and I tried it."

Rosie glanced over at Katrina who was leaning on the gate watching them. She waved for her to join them, but the girl shook her head. *I guess she and her fancy horse are too good for us.*

"What happened?" Carrie asked. "How did he become blind?"

"It was the summer I was fourteen. Dusty and I were at the county fair. I showed him in a jumping class, and we placed second, but the next day he crashed through one of the same jumps."

38

"Aw, poor boy," Jamie said.

Hannah looked as if she might cry as she remembered that day. "He had gone blind overnight."

Rosie was shocked. "That's awful. How can that happen?"

"Equine Recurrent Uveitis."

"Equine current what?" Jessie asked.

"ERU, that's easier," Hannah said. "It's a condition that can lead to blindness in horses. For some reason it's more common in Appaloosas than any other breed."

"Couldn't they do anything to fix it?" Jamie asked.

"No. In fact, the vet recommended that I euthanize him."

"What?" Rosie couldn't believe it. "You mean they wanted to kill him just because he was blind?"

"Yeah. I was pretty mad. No way I was going to let them kill my horse." Hannah leaned forward, put both arms around Dusty's neck, and hugged him. "I began training him to respond to voice commands. It took a while, but now Dusty can do everything he used to do before he went blind."

Jessie looked at her skeptically. "No way. You mean he can jump?"

"Yep." Hannah nodded. "Not as high, and it doesn't look pretty, but I tell him 'step up' and he jumps."

"Wow. I couldn't even walk with my eyes closed," Jamie said. "I can't imagine jumping."

"Maybe you all can watch us compete in the Extreme Cowboy Race at Equine Affaire next week."

"You and Dusty are going to be in the Extreme Cowboy Race?" Rosie looked incredulous. "Carrie and I watched it last year. We both want to be in it someday."

"You should," Hannah said. "But you have to be eighteen or over."

"I know." Rosie frowned. She didn't understand why she couldn't be in the race if she and Scamper could do everything that was required in the competition.

"I could enter Sassy," Billy said.

"They've had a few mules in it," Hannah said. "But you don't just enter. First you have to send in a video of you and your horse that shows the committee what you can do. They get entries from all over the country, and they use the videos to narrow the contestants down to about thirty for each competition."

"Wow! I can't believe you and Dusty got in," Rosie said.

Hannah smiled. "You haven't seen much of what he can do yet."

"Did you hear that, Katrina?" Jessie shouted. "Hannah and Dusty are going to be in the Extreme Cowboy Race! Do you want to go watch her with us?"

"I'll think about it." Katrina turned and walked away.

Everyone was quiet for a few moments, then Billy jumped off Sassy and tipped his cowboy hat toward the girls. "I need to get back to work. Thanks for letting me ride with you all." He walked across the arena and opened the gate. Sassy looked back and brayed to Dusty before she followed Billy out of the arena.

"Sassy really likes Dusty," Rosie said. "That's good. It will keep her away from my foal."

"Your foal?" Carrie eyed her sister. "You mean *our* foal."

"You have a foal?" Hannah asked.

Rosie nodded. "He's a nurse mare foal. We can show him to you after you put Dusty up."

Jessie hopped down from Patches and pulled her jeans back down over her boots. "What do you get if you win the cowboy race?"

Hannah smiled. "Three thousand dollars."

"Really?" Rosie's eyes widened.

"My fiancé and I are saving for a down payment on a house. Some of that prize money would sure help."

Rosie gulped. *Fiancé?*

"What's a fee-on-say?" Jessie asked.

"The person you're going to marry, silly." Rosie got off Scamper and walked beside Carrie toward the gate on the opposite side. When they were far enough away from the others, she glanced at her sister to see whether she was bothered by Hannah's news, but she couldn't read anything unusual in her expression. "Have you noticed Billy acting a little odd lately?"

"You mean William?" Carrie laughed. "Doesn't he always act a little odd?"

"So you haven't noticed anything different about him?"

Carrie thought for a moment and shook her head. "No, not really. Why?"

"Oh, nothing." Rosie slid the stall door open and led Scamper in. Maybe she was imagining things.

Chapter 6

Horse Shopping

The girls were up early the next morning. The sun looked like it was out to stay for a while, a welcome sight after several weeks of gray skies and rain. A perfect day for horse shopping. As soon as they finished their chores, Grandma was taking them to look at the red roan mare Rosie had seen advertised.

Rosie slid the barn door open. "I hope we can get Tilly. She sounded so cute."

"Don't let Grandma hear you say that," Carrie said. "Remember 1 Samuel 16:7?"

"I know. I know." Rosie grabbed a pitchfork and dropped it into the wheelbarrow. "Let's start with Baron's stall today. I want to have it finished before her royal highness gets here."

Carrie frowned. "I don't think you should call her names."

Rosie sighed. "I know. I've tried to be nice to her, but she acts like she's better than everyone else. And she's so bossy."

Rosie pushed Baron to the side so she and Carrie could clean. Baron moved over easily and began eating from his hay rack. He was a nice horse, Rosie had to admit. He was at least two hands taller than Scamper. She couldn't imagine having a horse that big. She wasn't counting on it, but maybe someday Katrina would let her ride him.

Carrie dumped a pitchfork full of shavings and manure in the wheelbarrow. "What happened to that tractor we talked about? If we get many more boarders, it's going to take forever to clean stalls with a wheelbarrow."

"We'll have to remind Dad about that," Rosie agreed.

When they were done, Rosie closed the stall door. "You take Cadence next, and I'll clean Dusty's."

When the girls finished their work on the boarders' side of the barn, they headed straight for Majestic's stall. "Let's turn him out with Kezzie," Rosie said.

The girls stood a while petting the foal. Since coming to Sonrise Stable, Majestic had grown even more attached to them. He whinnied whenever he heard them coming and every time they left him.

"I wish Jeremy would write to us so we could let him know how Majestic is doing," Carrie said.

"It's only been a week. He'll write soon. I'm sure. You know how much he loved Majestic."

"Sparky, you mean." Carrie smiled. She went to get Kezzie and led the older mare to the arena. Rosie followed with the colt.

After they turned them loose, Kezzie walked to the center, turned around a few times and dropped to the ground. She rolled over three times, then stood up and shook herself. Clouds of dust floated out from her back and sides. Majestic walked up to the mare and chomped his lips at her.

Rosie laughed. "He looks so weird when he does that."

Grandma had explained to them that the chomping was called "mouthing" or "clacking." Foals did it to remind older horses that they were small and helpless and not to hurt them.

"Maybe they think we look weird when we talk to each other," Carrie said.

Rosie started talking, opening her mouth in an exaggerated manner. "Do—you—think—I—look—weird—Majestic?"

The colt looked up at her.

Carrie laughed. "I don't know what he thinks, but I know you're weird!"

"Yes, but in an irresistible sort of way." Rosie grabbed the pitchfork that was leaning against the wall. "Let's get back to—"

"You little idiots!" Katrina bellowed from across the barn.

Rosie dropped the pitchfork, her heart pounding. "What? What did we do?"

Katrina jerked the gate open and stormed across the arena. "It's what you didn't do! I thought I told you to always check Baron's door to make sure it was latched."

Rosie looked at her sister, trying desperately to remember whether she had latched his stall door. Carrie was no help. She looked as if she were about to cry.

"Baron was wandering around in the aisle when I came into the barn—down by the mule and that freaky blind horse."

Rosie's mind flashed back to the awful day three years ago when her pony, Jet, had escaped from the barn and been killed. She was angry at Katrina for calling her an idiot and Dusty a freak, but she forced herself to apologize. "I'm sorry Katrina. It won't happen again."

"You got that right," Katrina huffed. "I'm going to get my dad to move Baron to another stable." She whirled around and stomped back across the arena.

Rosie felt all weak inside. "Mom and Dad and Grandma aren't going to be happy about this."

Kristy stood in front of the horse trailer signaling Grandma as she backed the truck. "Another foot," she yelled. Then she held her hand out flat. "Okay. That's good."

Grandma stopped and shut the truck off. They all watched Kristy crank the handle that lowered the trailer onto the truck hitch.

"Umm." Rosie scuffed her boot in the driveway.

Grandma studied her. "Umm, what?"

Rosie wondered whether Katrina had said anything to her mother or grandmother about Baron getting out of his stall. She knew she didn't want to make the long trip to look at the horse with her grandmother with this miserable feeling inside. It was best to get the confession over with. "Have either of you talked to Katrina?"

Kristy attached the safety chains and plugged the electric cord from the trailer into the truck. "Today, you mean? No. I haven't seen her."

Grandma shook her head. "I haven't talked to her either. Something wrong?"

Rosie took a deep breath. "Baron got out this morning."

"She yelled at us and called us idiots," Carrie added.

Kristy walked over and stood beside Grandma. "Well, you're not idiots. Forgetful maybe, but definitely not idiots." She smiled at her daughters. "I would give you a hug, but my hands are a mess." She tried to wipe the rust from the hitch off on her jeans. "Did you latch Baron's stall?"

Rosie scrunched her face and raised both hands palms up. "I don't know, Mom. I open and close stall doors so many times I don't even think about it. I think I did, but I'm just not sure."

"Did he get out of the barn?" Grandma asked.

Carrie shook her head. "No. Katrina said he was in the aisle."

Grandma looked at Kristy, then back to the girls. "Where was her dad?"

"He never comes in. He just drops her off and leaves," Rosie said.

Rosie saw a look pass between her mother and grandmother. Oh no. Maybe they weren't going to let her and Carrie go look at the horse.

Grandma stood thinking for a moment, then patted the side of the truck. "Okay, girls. Hop in."

Whew. Rosie sighed with relief. The bad feeling inside vanished. She and Carrie started toward the passenger door.

"Rosie," Grandma said.

She stopped and turned around.

"Thank you for being honest."

Rosie smiled and looked up at her grandmother. "Since we're taking the trailer, does that mean we're buying the horse today?"

"I don't know, but it never hurts to be prepared." Grandma winked at her.

Chapter 7

Tilly

After an hour's drive, they turned in at a tree-lined driveway. Grandma drove past the white farm house back to a small red barn where a small roan horse was tied to a rail, already saddled.

Grandma turned the truck off and frowned. "I don't like this."

"What? Grandma, we just got here." Rosie glanced at the horse. She looked every bit as pretty as she had imagined.

"I'd rather see her out in the field so I know how easy she is to catch and how she acts when saddled and bridled."

Carrie nodded. "Remember how hard Zach was to catch when I first got him?"

"But now he follows you around like a puppy dog," Rosie said.

The girls grabbed their riding helmets and jumped out of the truck. As the three walked toward the barn, a tall, wiry, middle-aged man came out to greet them.

He nodded at Grandma. "Howdy. Name's John."

Grandma smiled and introduced herself and the girls. "So this is Tilly?" Grandma walked around the mare looking her over. "Looks like you've ridden her."

"Just rode her 'round the yard a few times. Been a long time since I rode. Kinda miss it."

Rosie stared at the man. She had a feeling he wasn't telling the truth. It was obvious the horse had been ridden hard. Her flanks were covered with sweat, and her nostrils were enlarged. She was still breathing more rapidly than normal. Rosie looked at her grandmother and could tell she didn't believe him either.

Tilly was a beautiful horse. Her head was a solid reddish-brown. From her shoulders back, her color became lighter, almost pink, as more and more white hairs mingled in her coat.

Rosie stepped closer and reached out to pet her forehead. Tilly flinched, jerking her head away. She had a frightened look in her eye.

"I like to see a horse out in the field," Grandma said. "Do you mind if we start over? Let her out so we can catch her and saddle and bridle her ourselves?"

"Well—" John hesitated, fingering the stubble on his chin. "Umm—she'll prob'ly roll and git herself all dirty. She's real bad about that, and I just got 'er all cleaned up."

"That's okay. We've dealt with dirty horses before," Grandma said.

"Why don'cha hop on her right now?" John patted the saddle. "She's all ready for ya."

Grandma stood silently with her arms crossed, and Rosie knew she wasn't going to budge on this.

"All right." John stomped around to the left side of the horse, and Rosie saw Tilly tense all her muscles. He unfastened the girth and yanked the saddle off, setting it up on its horn on the ground. Next he untied her lead and practically dragged the poor animal toward the pasture. As they approached, a scruffy little chestnut pony stuck his head through the gate, begging for attention.

"Get outta the way, Charley." John swatted at him with the end of the lead rope. The pony sidestepped but didn't go far. When they were all inside the field, Charley quickly maneuvered himself between the girls. Rosie smiled at his persistence. She patted his neck absently and watched John unclip the lead from Tilly's halter. As soon as she realized she was free, the mare took off like a rocket, bucking and kicking. Rosie lost sight of her as she galloped up and over a hill.

Grandma frowned and shook her head. "Any point in me trying to catch her?"

John looked down at the ground and mumbled. "Took me an hour to catch her 'fore ya got here. Shoulda rode her when ya had the chance." He spat nasty brown tobacco juice on the ground. "She shore is pretty though, ain't she?"

Charley rubbed his head against Rosie, demanding more attention. She scratched his neck while keeping her eyes focused on her grandmother.

Grandma put her hands on her hips. "I told you I needed a horse for our summer camp! Do you know how far I drove to look at this horse? Why would you waste my time?"

"She's real good once ya get on 'er," John insisted.

"Yeah, I bet." Grandma shook her head. "Is that why you tried to wear her out before we got here?"

John leaned against the fence and changed the subject. He nodded toward the pony. "Looks like yer girls there have taken a real likin' to Charley."

Grandma slowly took a deep breath, then turned to look at the chestnut pony. Charley was about forty-six inches tall. His long, scraggly mane was so thick it split in two and flopped over to lie on both sides of his neck. His tail still had burrs in it from the previous autumn. He was thoroughly covered in mud and seemed to like it that way. What he lacked in appearance, however, he made up for in personality. He had clearly won Rosie and Carrie's hearts already.

Rosie scratched the pony's neck. "You would be perfect for little campers." She looked at her grandmother and could see a change come over her as she shifted into horse-trading mode.

"Has he been ridden?" Grandma asked.

"Everywhere." John nodded. "He even pulls a cart— well, from what I understand."

"How old?"

"Eight."

Grandma opened the pony's mouth. Rosie knew she was checking his teeth to determine whether he really was eight years old.

"Healthy?"

"As a horse." John nodded.

"How much?"

John hesitated as if he were trying to determine how much Grandma would pay. "A thousand dollars," he said firmly.

Grandma laughed. "You're dreaming."

"Seven-fifty?"

"Four hundred," Grandma offered.

"Five."

"Four-fifty," Grandma replied.

"You got it." He looked at her with grudging admiration and shook her hand. "You shore drive a hard bargain."

"I've done this a few times." Grandma smiled. "Before I make a final decision, though, we need to see whether this pony's everything you claim he is."

"I'll ride him," Rosie offered eagerly. It was a good thing John was too big to ride Charley. She was pretty certain Tilly was so fearful because of the way he treated her.

"If you don't mind," Grandma said, "we'll get him ready, and the girls will ride him."

"Shore thing." John went inside the barn and returned a few minutes later with Charley's halter and bridle. "Take yer time. I'll be in the barn if ya need me."

Grandma haltered the pony and held the lead as the girls groomed him. It was obvious Charley had not had this much attention in a long time, and he was soaking it up.

Rosie waved her hand in front of her face to keep the dirt and hair that was flying off him out of her mouth and eyes. Beneath the mud that caked his legs, she discovered white hairs. "Look, he has at least one white stocking."

"Keep digging," Grandma said, "you might uncover a few more."

Charley was the perfect gentleman as the girls saddled and bridled him. Rosie couldn't wait to try the pony out, but she decided to give Carrie the first chance. "Do you want to ride him?"

"Um, no." Carrie shook her head. "You go ahead."

Rosie strapped her helmet on, gathered the reins, and mounted. "Let go, Grandma. He's so short it won't be far to the ground if he does buck me off."

Grandma shook her head. "I'll lead you a bit first. I don't know how much, if anything, of what John told us is true. Charley seems well-trained, but it could be no one has ever been on this pony before."

Rosie felt awkward on the small pony after riding Scamper so much, and she hadn't been led around since she first started riding.

They walked down the drive and around the small yard once. Charley followed along obediently. When they returned to their starting point, Grandma unhooked the lead. "Okay, you're on your own."

Other than occasionally stopping to try to grab a bite of grass, the pony was perfectly behaved. "Let's see you trot," Grandma called.

Rosie squeezed her legs, and Charley picked up a trot, his short legs moving back and forth like pistons. Rosie laughed as she bounced. "A—bit—rough—er—than—Scamp—er."

She pushed the pony into a canter, a smoother three-beat gait. After a few trips around the yard, she hopped off and handed the reins to Carrie. "Your turn. He's kind of fun to ride!"

Rosie stood beside Grandma, watching her sister and Charley. "He seems so happy—like he's been waiting for us to come and rescue him from this place."

Grandma frowned. "I don't know. I'm having second thoughts."

"What?" Rosie whirled around to look at her grandmother. Hadn't she agreed to buy him? What had all the haggling with John over the price been about? Rosie could picture the younger kids at their summer camps having a ball with the pony.

"How can you not like him, Grandma? He's practically perfect."

Grandma tapped her open palm with the end of the lead rope and appeared to be deep in thought. "I'm just not sure. After all, he's not a red roan. Haven't you always told me that chestnut is your least favorite horse color?"

Ah. Grandma sure had a way of driving a lesson home. Rosie had been having so much fun with Charley; she hadn't given a thought to what color the pony was. She smiled. "You know, actually, chestnut is starting to grow on me."

Grandma smiled back at her. "Looks like we just bought a pony, then."

Chapter 8

Charley

"I can't believe she's still here," Rosie whispered to Carrie. She had spotted Katrina at her usual perch on the bench in front of the barn, phone in hand. Grandma stopped the truck and trailer in front of the stable. Rosie's stomach sank as she remembered Katrina yelling at them that morning.

"Oh, great," Carrie said as the girls climbed out of the truck.

Rosie grabbed the lead rope from the floor of the back seat. "I bet she'll love Charley."

The whole family materialized from somewhere in the barn and looked expectantly at Grandma and the girls.

"Well? Did you get the red roan mare?" Billy asked.

Rosie smiled and twirled the rope above her head. "Not exactly."

Jamie looked at the trailer. "You didn't buy anything?"

Jessie grabbed a metal slat on the side of the trailer and pulled herself up on the wheel well. "It's a pony! Grandma, you should have taken us with you. Why do Rosie and Carrie always get to do everything?"

"Next time," Grandma promised. "Let's get this pony into the barn."

Rosie opened the side door, and Charley whinnied. She backed the pony out of the trailer. Although they had spent considerable time cleaning him up, he still looked a bit rough around the edges.

"You've got to be kidding! Another misfit?" Katrina shook her head in disgust and walked into the barn.

Rosie rubbed Charley's neck. "Don't take it personally, boy. I don't think she likes any horses unless they're Thoroughbreds."

Charley shook his head as if to say he wasn't at all offended. He arched his neck and pranced in circles around Rosie.

Kristy walked over and patted the pony. "Well, that's certainly not what I expected you to come home with."

Eric closed and latched the trailer door. "This little guy might be perfect for kids who are afraid of the bigger horses. I remember how huge the horse seemed when I took my first ride."

"Yeah, but you were twenty-one then," Kristy laughed.

"You'd look pretty funny on Charley, Dad," Rosie teased.

"Okay, okay. So I didn't grow up as a cowboy." Eric scratched the pony's neck. "Stop ganging up on me."

"What happened with the mare?" Billy asked.

"Last we saw, she was galloping over a hill into the sunset." Grandma tossed her keys to Eric so he could park the trailer. "As scared as that horse looked, she may still be running."

"Mean people shouldn't be allowed to own horses," Rosie said. "I felt sorry for poor Tilly."

"Yes, so did I," Grandma agreed, "but if I bought every horse I ever felt sorry for, I'd be broke."

"What's his name?" Jamie asked.

Rosie made a theatrical bow, extending her arm toward the pony. "Everyone, meet Charley."

"Can I lead him?" Jessie begged.

Rosie handed the lead rope over to her cousin. Charley whinnied again, his head high and tail arched like an Arabian. Jessie led him down the aisle, letting him stop to greet Baron. Katrina rolled her eyes and backed away, refusing to touch him.

"Is your father picking you up?" Grandma asked. "You don't usually stay this late."

Katrina crossed her arms and leaned against Baron's stall. "He got tied up with work. He said he'll get here as soon as he can."

"We'll be eating supper right after we get the pony settled," Grandma said. "Why don't you join us?"

Katrina gave a shrug that wasn't really a yes or a no.

"Okay, boy. Let's get you into your stall." Jessie led the pony away from Baron.

There was a loud thud as Sassy butted her head against her stall door.

"Look out," Billy said. "She seems to think Charley's another foal in need of a mother."

Rosie opened the stall to the left of Cadence, and Jessie led the pony inside. Sassy ran from one side to the other, trying to see past Cadence into the pony's stall. She squealed and brayed, trying to get Charley's attention.

Cadence became so annoyed with her she kicked the wall between her stall and Sassy's.

"Are you ever going to teach your mule some manners?" Rosie asked.

"You guys are the ones who keep bringing new animals in here and making my mule all emotional." Billy tried to pet Sassy through the bars of the stall to calm her, but she paid no attention and continued to move frantically from side to side.

"You better watch out," Rosie warned. "You might get your arm broken."

Billy pulled his arm back out of the stall and frowned at the mule. "She'll wear herself out eventually, I guess."

The twins ran to get hay for Charley, and everyone else gathered at the front of his stall to watch him. He dropped to the floor and rolled in the fresh shavings. When he stood up, shavings clung to his mane and tail. He curled his upper lip as if he were smiling at them.

Grandma laughed. "I think he's trying to tell us that he likes it here."

Rosie patted her stomach. "What's for dinner, Mom? I'm starved."

Kristy put one arm around Rosie and the other around Carrie and hugged them. "There's a gi-normous pan of lasagna in the oven. I figured you would all be hungry when you got back."

"Mmm! Let's eat!" Rosie's mouth watered at the thought of her mother's lasagna. She was beyond hungry. It sounded like there was a dog-fight in her stomach with all the growling going on. She turned to leave the barn and saw a car pull up beside Grandma's truck. "Oh, no. Someone's here."

A woman and young girl stepped out and headed toward the barn.

Eric walked up to them. "Welcome to Sonrise Stable. I'm Eric."

"Hello. I'm Adrienne Smith, and this is my daughter, Jacqui."

After everyone had exchanged greetings, Grandma turned to Jacqui. "Do you have a horse you'd like to board with us?"

The girl smiled. "Not yet."

Adrienne nodded. "We hope to someday, though. My daughter loves horses. Ever since we heard you were having summer camps, she's been begging me to stop by and get her signed up."

"We're only having a few camps our first year, and we're already getting registrations, so it's good that you came out." Grandma turned to Rosie. "Why don't you girls show Jacqui around the barn while we take care of the paperwork?"

"Sure," Rosie said.

"Come with me, Adrienne." Grandma motioned toward the woman. "Everything's up at the house."

Rosie looked at Jacqui. The girl appeared to be about the same age as the twins, but she was a little shorter and very thin. "So you don't have your own horse?"

"No, but I'm saving up for one," Jacqui said. "I'm going to get a Thoroughbred."

"Oh, you like Thoroughbreds?" Rosie walked over to Baron's stall. "This is Katrina's horse, Baron. He's a Thoroughbred."

Katrina opened the stall door so Jacqui could pet him. "Baron won $200,000 on the track before he was retired five years ago," she said proudly. "I've owned him two years and am retraining him for dressage."

Jacqui was too short to reach Baron's head. The horse seemed to realize that and lowered his head so she could pet him. "My great-great-grandfather won the Kentucky Derby," she announced.

Rosie's mouth dropped open, and she stared at the girl.

"Yeah, right," Katrina laughed.

"He did," Jacqui insisted. "After that he raced in Russia and was the greatest jockey they ever had."

"Mm-hmm," Katrina laughed. "Hey, did I ever tell you guys about my great-great-grandmother who was the queen of England?"

Carrie frowned and tugged on Jacqui's arm. "Come on, you need to see the pony we bought today. You'll love him." The two girls took off for Charley's stall.

Rosie glared at Katrina. It was bad enough that she was mean to her and Carrie; she didn't have to be rude to their guests as well. She started to walk away, then stopped and turned around. "Why do you have to be so mean?"

Katrina sniffed. "Don't tell me you believe her? She's black. Since when have you ever seen a black jockey?"

Rosie wasn't sure what to think. She had never heard of a black jockey either, but that didn't prove Jacqui was lying.

Rosie turned and ran. She caught up with the other girls outside Charley's stall. "Was your grandfather really a jockey?"

Jacqui nodded. "He raced until he was fifty, then he had his own stable in France."

Fifty? Rosie couldn't imagine a jockey racing that long. That was almost as old as her grandmother. And a stable in France? Jacqui's story was becoming even more difficult to believe. She would have to ask her mom or grandmother about it later. "Come on. You have to see our nurse mare foal."

"What's a nurse mare foal?"

"I'll explain when we get over there." Rosie took off for the other side of the barn.

Chapter 9

Family Dinner

Katrina's father still hadn't arrived by the time Jacqui and her mother left. Rosie and Carrie found her curled up in a lawn chair in front of Baron's stall—her knees pulled up to her chest with her arms wrapped around them. The hood of her sweatshirt nearly covered her face. Her hands were hidden inside her sleeves, making it look as if she didn't have any.

Rosie tugged on her sweatshirt. "Is that you, Katrina?"

She and Carrie laughed, but Katrina just grunted.

Rosie persisted. "Grandma wants you to eat dinner with us."

"I don't know. I'll just wait here with Baron. My dad should be here soon." Katrina reached down on the opposite side of the chair and picked up a cat.

Rosie stared, dumbfounded. "June Bug?"

Katrina petted the bob-tailed calico that curled up in her lap. The cat began to purr loudly. "Is that her name?"

Rosie nodded. "She hates people. Watch out! She'll scratch or bite you. Grandma is the only one who's ever been able to hold her."

Katrina bent down and put her hands over June Bug's ears. "Poor kitty. Don't listen to those awful things she says about you."

June Bug rubbed her head against Katrina's hand and blinked her eyes.

"Unbelievable." Rosie shook her head. "Come on. Let's go in and eat. I'm starving."

"Our mom makes the best lasagna." Carrie tilted her head back and sniffed the air. "I think I can smell it from out here."

Katrina pinched her nose. "All I smell is that stinky mule."

Rosie was glad Scamper was on the other side of the barn so Katrina was less likely to make fun of him. She had to admit he was a little stinky at times. "Come on," she urged. "You have to be hungry. You've been here all day. And you look like you're freezing to death."

Katrina pulled her hood back and stared at the girls as if she had just realized they were sisters. "Are you twins?"

Rosie and Carrie looked at each other and laughed.

"We're twins born two months apart," Rosie said. She could tell Katrina was trying to figure out whether that was possible.

"And we're identical," Carrie laughed.

"Hah. I know that's not true," Katrina said.

"You're right," Carrie admitted. "I was adopted about six months ago."

"Really?"

Rosie studied Katrina. "What did you think we were? How else could two sisters be so close in age?"

"I guess I never thought about it," Katrina said.

"When is your mom coming out to the stable?" Carrie asked.

Katrina didn't answer. She pulled her hood up again and slumped back in the chair.

There was an awkward silence for several moments. Rosie could tell Carrie was sorry she had asked the question. "Come on, Katrina." She tugged on her arm again. "Let's go eat."

Katrina slowly set June Bug on the ground and stood up. "Okay. I am kind of hungry."

It was a good thing the old farmhouse was large. They didn't often all eat together, but tonight everyone was there. It reminded Rosie of their Thanksgiving dinner the previous fall. Carrie, their mom and dad, Grandma, Julie and Jonathan and their three kids, Billy, and now Katrina. Rather than turkey and dressing, though, the air was filled with the aroma of homemade lasagna and garlic bread. Rosie's mouth watered. There was nothing like a horse-buying trip to work up an appetite.

When Katrina came in with the girls, Grandma smiled and grabbed an extra plate from the cupboard. She set it down on the table. "Make room for one more."

Everyone shifted around to make a spot for Katrina. Eric went to get another chair. When they were all seated, he prayed and Kristy started the lasagna around the table. There was a loud buzz as everyone began talking at once.

Rosie forgot about Katrina and jumped into the conversation. "Grandma, Jacqui said her great-great-grandfather was a jockey and that he won the Kentucky Derby."

"She said he raced in Russia," Carrie said between bites.

Jessie didn't bother to wait until she had finished chewing. "And he had a stable in France," she said with a mouthful of lasagna.

"Really?" Grandma looked surprised. "She told you all that? That's funny; her mother didn't mention anything about it."

"It would be easy enough to find out if it's true," Kristy said. "There has to be a record of all the Kentucky Derby winners."

"What was her great-great-grandfather's name?" Grandma asked.

Rosie shrugged. "I don't think she said."

"Finished the girls' bunkhouse today," Billy announced proudly. "It's ready for campers."

"It took you long enough," Rosie teased.

"Yeah, well, if I would've had some help, it might have gone faster, but on second thought, having seen how you two hammer—maybe not."

"Humph! Carrie and I had more important things to do—like helping Grandma buy horses."

"How is the little runt doing anyway?"

Jessie elbowed Billy. "Charley is not a runt."

"I'm sure he'll be a favorite with the campers," Rosie said.

"Speaking of campers, Jacqui makes ten signed up already, and we haven't even advertised yet," Kristy said.

"Guess who called to sign up today?" Grandma asked Rosie.

"I have no idea."

"Just guess," Grandma prodded.

Rosie racked her brain, trying to think of who it might be. She looked at Carrie, who shook her head. She knew Grandma wouldn't be satisfied until she guessed. "Umm, Emily?"

Grandma looked at her with a blank expression.

"Remember? She gave the demonstration at the 4-H club on the evolution of the horse."

"Ah, yes, now I remember. Good guess, but no, it wasn't Emily."

Rosie looked at her grandmother, hoping she wasn't going to make her continue guessing. Fortunately, Grandma seemed anxious to reveal her surprise.

"Jeremy!" Grandma announced with a big smile.

Rosie jumped up out of her chair. "Jeremy? You're kidding! Jeremy's coming to our camp?"

"Yippee," Billy clapped, then turned to Rosie. "Who's Jeremy?"

She punched him in the arm. "Jeremy's father owns the nurse mare farm where Majestic was born. Majestic was Jeremy's horse's foal."

"But he called him Sparky," Carrie said.

Rosie sat back down. "That's why we decided his full name would be Majestic Spark."

"Wow, one boy. We need to get more signed up," Jared said. "Aren't all the other campers so far girls?"

Grandma nodded. "There is definitely something about girls and horses."

"You going to help me start on the boys' bunkhouse tomorrow?" Billy asked Jared.

"Sure."

"They don't need a bunkhouse," Rosie said. "Jeremy could bring his sleeping bag and sleep in Majestic's stall."

"He'd probably like that," Carrie agreed.

Rosie had almost forgotten about Katrina, who had been silent since she entered the house. Everyone in Rosie's family talked a lot, and dinner conversations often went in a dozen different directions at the same time. Even Carrie, who used to be shy, now talked almost as much as everyone else. Rosie looked across the table at Katrina. "How do you like the lasagna?"

She was surprised to see Katrina smile. Rosie wasn't sure she'd ever seen her do anything but frown.

"It's great. My dad's not much of a cook so we don't have real meals too often."

"Would you like to go to Equine Affaire with us next week?" Grandma asked. "We're all going to watch Hannah and Dusty compete in the Extreme Cowboy Race."

"Uh, okay. I guess I don't have anything else to do."

"It's so much fun," Rosie said. "They have horses of every kind, clinics, and lots of places to buy horse stuff."

"My favorite part is the race," Carrie said.

"Me too," Rosie agreed. "I'm going to be in it someday."

"You've got a few years before you can do that," Kristy said.

"I know. Carrie and I are going to be in the state 4-H trail ride this fall, though. That's a start."

"You better start conditioning that fat pony of yours if you're going to compete in a trail ride," Billy said.

"Fat?" Rosie replied indignantly. "Have you looked at your mule lately?"

"Yeah," Carrie joined in. "When's the baby due?"

Billy laughed. "Sassy and I would be famous then, wouldn't we? Okay, I admit she could stand to lose some weight."

"As soon as the trails are dry enough, we could all start training together," Rosie suggested.

Billy and Carrie nodded.

"Does anyone know if Hannah needs help with Dusty at Equine Affaire?" Billy asked. "I thought I could help her before the race."

"She already has help," Rosie blurted out.

Billy looked at her. "How do you know?"

"I think I remember her saying she did. Didn't she, Carrie?" Rosie gave Carrie a look that was meant to get her to agree, but Carrie just looked back at her blankly.

"I'll ask her tomorrow," Billy said.

Chapter 10

The Escape

Charley ran around the arena. He was so much fun to watch. His head and tail were high in the air as if he thought he were part Arabian. Perhaps somewhere in the distant past he had an Arabian ancestor. There was something about the pony's attitude—mischievous, but loving—that made everyone smile. Everyone except Katrina.

Rosie had thought Katrina was beginning to like Sonrise Stable. She had been almost nice when she joined them for dinner last week, but now she seemed more irritable than ever. As Rosie passed Baron's stall on the way to the arena, Katrina had asked her if she could get Dusty, Sassy, and Charley together so she could take a photo of the misfits to send to her friends in Florida.

Somehow it was all right for Rosie to criticize Sassy, but it annoyed her when Katrina did—and it made her downright angry when she made fun of Dusty and Charley. If you asked Rosie, Katrina was the one who was a misfit.

Katrina was at the barn every afternoon and evening, and on nonschool days her father often left her at the stable all day. Rosie had to admit that she was a very good rider. It was obvious that she loved her horse, and they communicated effortlessly. Rosie liked to watch her when she trained Baron. Recently she had been working on trotting diagonally across the arena. Grandma had explained

73

that in dressage, that was called a half-pass. Rosie wanted to train Scamper to do that too, but she wasn't sure how to get started.

Carrie brought Majestic into the arena, interrupting Rosie's thoughts. The foal and Charley had formed a strong bond. They loved to be out together. Charley seemed to sense that the foal wasn't strong enough to play roughly with yet. Rosie watched the pony take off across the arena with Majestic following after him as if they were playing tag.

"Dusty's loose!"

The panic in Katrina's voice caused the hair to stand up on the back of Rosie's neck. She and Carrie sprinted across the arena and out the front door of the barn.

Rosie spotted the blind horse halfway down the driveway, walking straight toward the road. Her mind raced. Other than cleaning his stall, she hadn't been around him much. Would he be frightened if she approached him? How could she catch him? He didn't even have a halter on.

She barked out orders. "Carrie, go get Grandma! Katrina, run back to the barn and get a halter and lead rope!"

They took off in different directions, while Rosie ran toward the road, making a wide arc around Dusty. When she reached the end of the drive, she grabbed the gates and pulled them shut, fastening the chain around the bars. *Whew! At least Dusty wouldn't be able to get out on the road now.*

Rosie looked back and was relieved to see Grandma and Carrie coming out of the house. Katrina had a head start on them from the barn.

"Everyone spread out," Grandma called out, "so we're surrounding him."

They moved apart, each approaching the horse from a different direction.

"Talk to him and move slowly, girls," Grandma said. "The last thing we want is for him to get scared and run."

"Easy boy," Rosie said. "You're all right."

Dusty stopped to snatch a bite of grass along the side of the driveway. He raised his head, chewing and flicking his ears back and forth like an antenna to pick up their voices.

Rosie looked around her. Things that normally seemed harmless now loomed like dangerous obstacles—the ditch, the trees in the yard, the fence, and the twins' bikes they had left in the grass a few days ago. One misstep and Dusty might injure himself.

They began to gradually close in on the horse. Rosie could hear the others talking to him.

"Whoa, Dusty."

"That's a boy."

"Easy, buddy."

Dusty nervously turned his head from side to side as if searching for the familiar voice of his master, the one he trusted to be his eyes.

Rosie was the closest to Dusty now. She held out a hand toward the gelding, then, realizing he couldn't see her at all, she dropped her hand to her side, clutching nervously at her pant leg. Something crinkled in her pocket—the peppermint she had saved for Scamper. She fished it out of her jeans.

"Here, boy. Do you like peppermints as much as Scamper does?"

She was close enough that the crinkling of the cellophane as she unwrapped the mint caught Dusty's attention. He turned in her direction, his nostrils quivering as he inhaled the peppermint scent. He stretched his head toward her. Rosie looked past him to see where the others were.

"Hurry up, Katrina. I almost have him." She extended her hand, and Dusty's lips gently brushed her palm. He picked up the mint and crunched it loudly.

Katrina stepped up on the other side and wrapped a lead rope around him. She pushed the halter toward Rosie under Dusty's neck. Rosie slipped the halter on his head as the horse breathed warm peppermint breath in her face.

Grandma heaved a sigh of relief as she and Carrie reached them. "Thank God he wasn't hurt. Come on; let's get him back to the barn." She patted Dusty and took the lead rope from Rosie.

When the gelding was safely in his stall, Grandma turned to face the girls. "What is going on around here? First Baron gets out, and now Dusty. How can we run a boarding stable if you keep letting the horses out?"

Rosie hung her head, not wanting to look her grandmother in the eye.

"Do you know how dangerous it is for a blind horse to be out wandering around in an area he's not familiar with?"

Rosie and Carrie nodded. Katrina turned and walked off toward Baron's stall.

Grandma watched her leave but didn't say anything.

"This time I'm almost positive I latched his stall door," Rosie said.

Grandma softened a bit. "I want to believe you, but how did he get out, then?"

Rosie didn't have an answer for that.

"I noticed you shut the front gates, Rosie. That was quick thinking," Grandma said. "I'm proud of you. Even though there's not much traffic out here, it could have been very bad if he had gotten out on the road."

Rosie didn't want to think about that. Dusty was safe, and tomorrow he and Hannah would compete in the cowboy race. Her heart sank as she realized their punishment might be not being allowed to go to Equine Affaire. She looked at her grandmother, almost afraid to ask. "Can we still go tomorrow?"

Grandma wrapped an arm around each of them and hugged them to her. "Yes. I believe in 'innocent until proven guilty,' but after Equine Affaire your mom and dad and I will discuss what needs to change around here to make sure this never happens again. Now why don't you two run and open the gates so people can get in and out?"

That afternoon, Hannah arrived to bathe Dusty and get him ready for Equine Affaire. Rosie cringed when Grandma began telling her about Dusty's escape that morning. She didn't seem to be mad, just relieved that he was okay.

Hannah led the Appaloosa out of the barn to the wash rack. Rosie, Carrie, and Billy followed, carrying buckets, sponges, shampoo, and towels.

"Are you nervous?" Rosie asked.

"Kind of," Hannah admitted. "We've been to a lot of shows, but never to anything this big before."

"You'll do great." Rosie was anxious to see what Dusty could do. It had been so cool and rainy, she hadn't seen Hannah ride him anywhere except in the indoor arena, and then mostly at a walk or trot.

"What time is the competition?" Carrie asked.

Hannah hosed down Dusty's legs. "The race starts at three in the coliseum."

"We're leaving early in the morning," Rosie said. "We'll make sure we're in the coliseum by 2:45. I wouldn't miss the race for anything."

"You'll have a big cheering section," Carrie added.

Hannah smiled. "Thanks. Dusty will appreciate that."

"Too bad Sassy can't go and watch him," Rosie laughed. "She'd cheer louder than anyone."

"Yeah, that's something my mule's good at—making noise." Billy handed Hannah the bottle of shampoo. "Um. Do you, uh—" He fiddled with the towel he was holding. "Do you need help getting Dusty there tomorrow? I mean, I could take the day off and help you."

Rosie watched Billy's face turn red.

Hannah shook her head. "I'm taking him there today as soon as I'm done bathing him."

"Oh?" Billy scuffed his boot in the gravel. "Well, I could help today too."

"Thanks, William. You're so kind, but my fiancé should be here anytime now. We're driving up there together."

Oh, no. Rosie could almost feel Billy's pain.

He stared blankly at Hannah. "Your fiancé?"

She stepped behind Dusty and sudsed his tail. "Yes, that's why Dusty is here right now. My parents sold their house, so I needed a place to keep him until Cody and I find a place of our own."

"Oh." Billy nodded and turned away.

Hannah rinsed the soap out of Dusty's tail with the hose.

"Umm, I just remembered something I have to do." Billy dropped the towel on the ground and trudged back toward the barn.

Chapter 11

Equine Affaire

The entire family was up at dawn the next morning, helping with the chores so they could get an early start on their trip. Rosie's father, Eric, and her uncle, Jonathan, had both taken the day off work so they could go with the rest to Equine Affaire.

"Are you sure you don't want to go?" Eric asked Billy.

"No, no." Billy shook his head. "Someone has to keep an eye on things around here."

"Come on," Rosie begged. "You should come with us."

"No, really, I'm fine. Sassy and I are going to start training for next year's race."

"Thanks, Billy," Eric said. "We'll be back sometime this evening."

Rosie frowned as she watched Billy return to the barn. Carrie tugged on her arm, and Rosie turned to follow her and Katrina to Grandma's truck. Everyone else piled into Julie and Jonathan's van.

"We should take the trailer, Grandma," Rosie said. "I'm sure we could find a few horses to buy while we're there."

"You're probably right," Grandma laughed, "but I doubt that we could afford them."

They traveled for a half-hour on narrow country roads, then Grandma turned onto the entrance ramp of the freeway. "Oh, girls, remember what Jacqui told you about her great-great-grandfather?"

Rosie nodded.

"I gave her mother a call." Grandma turned to see whether any traffic was coming and merged onto the freeway.

Rosie leaned forward. "What did you find out?"

"It's all true. In fact, it's even more amazing than Jacqui said."

"You're kidding," Katrina said.

Rosie turned to look at her. She was trying to stay positive, but she kind of wished Grandma hadn't invited Katrina to come along.

"Let me see if I can remember everything she told me. His name was James Winkfield. He was born in Kentucky not long after the Civil War, the youngest of eighteen children."

"Eighteen?" Rosie gasped. "I can't imagine having that many kids."

Grandma laughed. "Yes, I have a hard enough time keeping track of my six grandchildren." She thought for a moment. "His nickname was Wink, and he began racing at the age of fifteen."

"That's almost the same age as me," Katrina said.

"And he did win the Kentucky Derby—twice in fact," Grandma continued. "In 1901 and 1902. A black jockey hasn't won the Derby since then."

"I never knew there were any black jockeys," Rosie said.

Grandma nodded. "I didn't realize that either, so I did some research. In the first Derby, thirteen of the fifteen jockeys were black. I believe black riders won fifteen of the first twenty-eight Derbies."

"Why was he the last black jockey to win the Derby?" Carrie asked. "If they were so good at racing, what happened to them?"

"In the time before the Civil War, slaves were used as jockeys because they didn't have to be paid. After the war, as horse racing became more popular and more money could be won, white riders wanted to become jockeys."

"So they started winning more than the black jockeys?" Rosie asked.

"Yes, but not always honestly. From what I read, the white riders would bump the black jockeys' horses in a race or whip them. Sometimes they would even put their feet under a black rider's stirrup and try to flip him out of the saddle."

"That's awful," Carrie said.

"That's why Wink went to race in Europe and Russia. He didn't face the prejudice there that he did in the United States. He was considered one of the best jockeys ever, winning many of the biggest races in Russia. And he did have his own stable later in France, where he and his son raised and trained racehorses."

So it was all true. Rosie felt bad for doubting Jacqui. No wonder the girl had been so excited about getting a Thoroughbred someday. She tapped her grandmother on the shoulder. "Are we related to anyone famous?"

Grandma laughed. "No, not that I'm aware of."

Rosie couldn't wait until summer camp so she could ask Jacqui more about her grandfather. She glanced over at Katrina, wondering how she felt about being wrong, but the girl just stared out the window. Rosie sighed. It would have been more fun if Billy had come along and Katrina had stayed behind at the stable.

Despite being excited about the trip, Rosie wasn't used to getting up so early. She tried unsuccessfully to hold back a big yawn. As the conversation died out, the vibration of the truck made her sleepy. She wadded her jacket up into a pillow, leaned against the truck door and dozed.

The family gathered together outside the coliseum to plan their day at Equine Affaire. All around them people were leading or riding horses of every breed and color. Horse and barn smells mingled with the aroma of food from the long line of concession stands. Rosie glanced at her watch. It wasn't quite ten o'clock, but her stomach was already complaining. She looked over at her mom. *Was it too early to ask her parents about lunch?*

Rosie turned to watch a tall, black horse with a long, wavy mane and tail that was coming up behind them. She pointed. "Look, Carrie. There's a Friesian."

Grandma handed Rosie a schedule of events. "What do you want to see first?"

Rosie scanned the schedule. "Trick training! I want to see that." Her mind made up, she folded the paper and stuck it in the back pocket of her jeans.

"That sounds like fun," Grandma agreed. "Who wants to go with us?"

The twins walked over and stood beside Rosie, Carrie, and Grandma.

Grandma looked at Katrina. "Would you like to join us?"

She shrugged as if horse tricks were beneath her dignity. "I'm not really into that kind of thing, but I guess I'll go."

Eric, Jonathan, and Jared went off to look at trucks and horse trailers. Julie and Kristy decided to watch a clinic on barrel racing.

Grandma looked sternly at the twins, especially Jessie. "Don't wander off. I don't want to lose you."

Jessie held up her hands. "Why are you looking at me?"

Grandma shook her head. "I can't imagine."

The group started off, making their way through the crowd to Cooper Arena for the trick training clinic. They climbed the steps and found seats together in the top row as the clinic was starting.

A man in a straw cowboy hat, black chaps, and a red-checked shirt entered the arena followed by a beautiful palomino with a gleaming white mane and tail. "Are you happy to see everyone this morning, Rocky?"

The horse nodded his head up and down repeatedly, and the crowd laughed.

"Ready to show everyone what you can do?"

Rocky nodded again. Rosie noticed that the horse wasn't wearing a halter. He was totally controlled by the man's voice or some other signals that she couldn't see.

The man walked toward a wooden pedestal about two feet tall. Rocky stepped up onto the pedestal with both front feet and posed for the audience.

Rosie elbowed Carrie and whispered, "Scamper could do that. He loves to stand on things."

At another signal Rocky jumped up so all four feet were on the pedestal. He slowly turned around, carefully positioning each hoof on the small surface, then he stepped down.

"Let's play ball." The man rolled a giant ball toward Rocky. The horse lifted a front leg to kick it back to him. After the horse kicked the ball a few times, the man tossed it up in the air. Rocky butted it with his head, soccer-style. The crowd clapped.

"I think everyone liked your ball playing, Rocky. Why don't you take a bow?" The palomino stretched one front leg forward and knelt down on the other. When the horse stood back up, he reached over and grabbed the man's hat in his teeth, pulling it off his head.

"Hey, give that back!" When the man reached for his hat, Rocky moved his head up and down so the hat was always just out of the man's reach.

Rosie laughed. She glanced over at Katrina and saw that she was at least smiling.

Rocky dropped the hat on the ground. When the man bent down to pick it up, the horse grabbed a large red handkerchief out of his back pocket.

The man shook his head. "You're wearing me out, Rocky. I think it's time for a nap."

The two walked over to a tarp on the ground. Rocky knelt down, then plopped over on his side, lying on the tarp as if it were his bed. The man brought a pillow and slipped it under Rocky's head, then he placed a sheet over the horse's hindquarters.

Rocky reached back, grabbed the sheet in his teeth, and pulled it up over himself like a blanket. He laid his head on the pillow and closed his eyes.

When the crowd finished clapping, the horse raised his head and pulled his legs up under him, but he didn't stand. The man sat on his back, and then Rocky stood up. They cantered around the outside of the ring, bareback without a bridle or even a halter on the horse. The man took off his hat and waved it to the crowd as he rode past, which caused everyone to cheer more loudly.

"I can't wait to get home and try this stuff!" Rosie said to Carrie.

Next, the man briefly explained how to get started with trick training, covering a few of the more basic tricks. Rosie listened attentively so she would know what to do when she started to work with Scamper. Maybe she could get Billy to build a pedestal for her, since that seemed like the easiest thing for Scamper to learn first.

When the clinic was over, they went through the Breed Pavilion, a large horse barn with informational booths for just about every breed of horse and even several that Rosie hadn't heard of, like the Gypsy Vanner and the Nakota Horse.

They watched another clinic, this one on vaulting. Rosie had never heard of that either, but once she saw it, she wanted to try vaulting as well. A team of three girls performed gymnastics on a large draft horse as he cantered a circle around them. They leaped onto him, performing handstands and other moves on his back, then flipped off to the ground.

"I could do that," Rosie said.

"Yeah, right. You can't even do that stuff on the ground, let alone on a horse," Carrie laughed.

After the vaulting demonstration, they ate lunch and shopped in the merchant building. Rosie had never seen so much horse equipment in one place before. There was booth after booth of saddles, boots, show outfits, and anything horse related you could imagine. She had five dollars in her pocket to spend, but so far she hadn't seen anything even close to that price.

Rosie checked her watch every five or ten minutes. She didn't want to miss Hannah's event. At 2:40 she announced, "It's time. Let's go to the coliseum." Even though she wasn't competing, she felt a few butterflies fluttering around in her stomach for Hannah and Dusty.

Outside the coliseum, horses and riders were gathering for the competition. Rosie spotted Hannah and Dusty and hurried over to them. The rest of the family was already there, wishing them well.

Rosie noticed a tall young man with short, black hair standing next to Dusty. She figured he had to be Hannah's fiancé, Cody. Seeing him reminded her of Billy. She felt sad for a moment and wondered what he was doing back home. Rosie turned and looked up at Hannah. "How's Dusty? Is he ready?"

"I think so. He doesn't seem nervous. I rode him in the coliseum last night, so I think he'll be okay."

Rosie reached into her pocket and pulled out a mint. She unwrapped it and held it out to Dusty. "Here, boy. This will give you extra energy." After he had taken it, she patted him encouragingly. "You're going to beat them all."

She put her hand back in her pocket and fingered the other two mints she was saving to give him after he won the race.

Chapter 12

Extreme Cowboy Race

At the center of the arena, the family found seats halfway up the bleachers. Rosie sat down with Carrie on her right and Katrina on her left. "Perfect. I can see everything from here." She tapped her dad on the shoulder. "You have the camera, Dad?"

Eric, sitting in the row in front of her, pulled a video camera out of the camera bag and waved it at her.

"Don't forget to record Hannah and Dusty."

He nodded.

Rosie looked down at the course and tried to figure out what the contestants would have to do.

Although it was called the Extreme Cowboy Race, it wasn't a typical race. The horses wouldn't run against each other. It was like a trail class, only with more difficult obstacles. The fact that it was timed made it even more challenging. If two contestants scored the same on the obstacles, whoever had the faster time would win. The top ten finishers from this round would compete again tomorrow on a totally different course to determine the final winners.

"Hmm. They must start at that gate, then go to the barrels." Rosie looked to her left. "But where do they go after that?"

Katrina eyed her. "Are you going to chatter like that through the whole competition?"

Rosie hadn't even realized she had been talking out loud. "Yep, probably. Except when it's Hannah and Dusty's turn; then I'll be yelling." Rosie smiled broadly and turned her attention back to the arena. She wasn't going to let Katrina's attitude spoil the day for her.

Finally a group of people entered the ring—the announcer, the timer, two judges, and several people who would reset any obstacles that were moved by the competitors. They called all the riders in, without their horses, and walked through the course, explaining what needed to be done to successfully complete each obstacle.

"I don't think I could remember all that," Carrie said. "What happens if they don't do the course in the right order?"

"They take points off," Rosie said.

"I still don't think Dusty can jump." Katrina sat back in her seat, resting her chin on her fist as if she were bored.

Rosie pointed to three sets of barrels in the center of the ring. "I guess we'll find out. They have to jump over those."

The first contestant entered the arena—a man on a large bay Quarter Horse. The announcer informed the audience that this team had finished second in last year's race. Rosie watched as he went through obstacle after obstacle almost perfectly. The horse was fast too.

"What a great start to the Extreme Cowboy Race!" the announcer said at the end of the run. He congratulated the rider. "Looks like we'll be seeing you again tomorrow."

The contestant tipped his hat and trotted his horse out of the ring.

Rosie felt a little discouraged. That team would be hard to beat. She grew restless as several more contestants went through the course. She kept looking over the doors at the left end of the arena to see if she could spot Hannah and Dusty waiting to enter. "When is it going to be Hannah's turn?"

Katrina turned to Rosie and held her finger up to her lips. "Shh."

The obstacle that caused the most trouble for the horses was a narrow L-shaped chute made of round pen panels. The horses had to back through the chute. The horse that was currently in the arena seemed especially afraid of it. He was partway through when his hindquarters banged against one side, causing the chute to move. The movement frightened him even more.

Rosie couldn't tell for sure, but it looked like the rider's foot or stirrup was caught on a panel. The next thing she knew, the panels, the horse, and the rider were all on the ground. She gasped and covered her eyes. Seconds later she felt someone tapping her leg.

"They're okay," Carrie said.

Rosie slowly opened her eyes and saw that the horse was on his feet, apparently unharmed. The rider got back on and rode out of the arena as the crowd applauded.

"Our next rider is Hannah on her Appaloosa gelding, Dusty," the announcer called out.

A loud whoop went up from the Sonrise Stable section. Rosie stood up and yelled until Katrina grabbed her arm and pulled her back into her seat.

Hannah led Dusty to the side wall of the arena and turned to look at the announcer.

"On your mark ... Get set ... Go!"

Hannah mounted quickly and started the initial lap to the left around the outer wall of the coliseum. Dusty cantered, moving much slower than the previous contestants.

A woman behind Rosie leaned forward and yelled practically in her ear. "What is she doing out there? This is a race, not a western pleasure class!"

Rosie bristled and turned to face her. "Do you know that horse is blind?"

"What?" The woman's mouth dropped open, and she quietly sat back in her seat.

Rosie turned her attention to the race. Hannah was getting her lasso out to try to rope a fake steer head that was sitting on a bale of straw. The rope fell short. "It's okay. You'll do better on the next one," Rosie called out.

Next they had to canter to one side, stop, and do a rollback, wheeling around to face the other direction. Dusty was too excited. He kept throwing his head in the air and fighting the bit.

Rosie held her breath as they approached the back-through chute. Hannah stopped Dusty and turned around, maneuvering him so his hindquarters were right in front of the opening. He reared a little, not wanting to back into whatever that awful thing was behind him. She got him settled down, and he backed all the way through.

"Whew!" Rosie sighed. "He did that better than any of them have so far."

They performed well at the next two obstacles also—standing inside a box made of wooden poles where Hannah had to dismount and remount, and then drag a log both forward and backward with a rope.

Next were the jumps. Rosie knew this would be the most difficult for Dusty. There were three sets of barrels, two in each set, laid end-to-end on their sides. Hannah urged Dusty forward until his front legs touched the first set of barrels. Rosie couldn't hear her, but she saw Hannah's mouth moving and knew she was telling Dusty, "Step up."

Rosie was amazed as she watched Dusty jump nearly straight up in the air, clearing the barrels easily with his front legs but hitting them with his backs. He didn't do quite as well at the next two jumps, but Rosie was so proud of him she thought her heart would explode.

"Oh, by the way, in case you haven't heard," the announcer said, "this horse is totally blind."

A gasp went through the crowd, and everyone cheered for Dusty's brave attempt at jumping the barrels. Rosie, once again, was on her feet yelling wildly. This time Carrie reached out and pulled her back into her seat.

The next few obstacles were a blur to Rosie. She kept thinking about how brave Dusty was to jump into the unknown for Hannah. Next thing she knew, they were picking up a set of weighted bags from off the top of a barrel. Hannah draped the bags over Dusty's withers, and they walked over to a canopy with three rows of streamers hanging down. She had to get Dusty to side-pass through the obstacle.

Although he couldn't see them, Dusty could surely feel the streamers touching his head and back. He must have wondered what they were, but he side-passed obediently all the way through. It was his best obstacle so far.

Hannah dropped the bags off on top of another barrel, then turned Dusty toward the outside of the arena for the final lap. Dusty broke into a canter to the right, then picked up speed until he was running at a full gallop around the ring, trusting Hannah to be his eyes.

Rosie jumped up, yelling at the top of her lungs and shaking her fist in the air. "Go, Dusty! Atta boy!" This time Carrie and Katrina joined her. Soon the entire crowd was on their feet, cheering for Hannah and Dusty.

Everyone remained standing as the two crossed the finish line. Rosie looked at Katrina and was surprised to see tears running down her cheeks. *What was she crying about?*

The announcer gave Dusty's time. Rosie realized it was one of the slowest so far, but Hannah and Dusty were definitely a hit with the crowd. She smiled when she noticed her grandmother in front of her pulling tissues out of her pocket. She could never understand it, but her grandmother cried almost as much when she was happy as when she was sad.

The announcer walked over to talk to Hannah, and the crowd took their seats.

"We've never had a horse blind in both eyes in the competition before. What a brave horse! Isn't this horse amazing?"

The crowd cheered again.

"How did you and Dusty get started?"

Hannah's voice was shaky from the excitement or nervousness or maybe both. "He was my first horse. He went blind at age nine, and the vet asked me if I wanted to euthanize him. You don't tell a stubborn fifteen-year-old to put her horse down. I was determined to bring him back to what we used to do."

Rosie could tell that the announcer was becoming a little emotional. He paused a moment to collect himself. "Well, I love Dusty, and I love you. We're proud of you, cowgirl!" He shook her hand, and Hannah led Dusty out of the arena.

The announcer stood, watching her leave. "That'll tug at your old heartstrings, won't it?"

Rosie and her family watched a few more contestants, then everyone hurried to the barn where Dusty was stalled. There was a huge crowd gathered around, congratulating Hannah and asking her all kinds of questions. There were even reporters from several newspapers and magazines.

Rosie knew they wouldn't qualify for the second round, but somehow that didn't seem important anymore. She pulled the mints out of her pocket, unwrapped one, and handed the other to Carrie. Dusty had a good nose. He turned toward Rosie, and she offered him the treat. She petted him as he crunched the mint. "If I were the judge, I would have given you first place!"

After he finished the first mint, he nudged Carrie, and she fed him the second.

"Aw, thanks, girls," Hannah said. "I see you've discovered that he likes mints. Who needs an old trophy or ribbon anyway when you can have peppermints?"

Rosie was happy that everyone had seen how special Dusty was, and of course that was because Hannah had believed in him when no one else did. They made the perfect team. She hoped that someday she could communicate that well with Scamper and that he would trust her as much as Dusty trusted Hannah.

They took in a few more exhibits at Equine Affaire, then Grandma and the girls headed to the truck for the long trip home. Rosie was exhausted. She climbed into the back seat after Carrie and Katrina and pulled the door shut. Katrina had been unusually quiet all evening. She looked like she didn't feel well. All Rosie needed was for her to get car sick on the way home. "Are you okay?"

Katrina shook her head and looked down. "No."

Grandma turned around. "What' s wrong?"

"I didn't mean for him to get out!" she sobbed.

Grandma looked confused. "For who to get out?"

"Dusty."

"What?" Sparks flashed in Rosie's eyes. "You let him out?"

"I only wanted him to be out in the aisle. I heard you and Carrie in the arena and thought you were coming over to my side of the barn." Katrina sniffed and wiped the tears from her eyes with her hand. "I ran back and opened Dusty's door, then went into Baron's stall and started brushing him. I thought the two of you would come in and find him out in the aisle."

Rosie stared at her, not understanding.

"I didn't think he would go anywhere, but the next thing I knew he was headed out the front door, and I couldn't stop him."

"You let him out?" Rosie repeated. "And you blamed it on me and Carrie?"

Katrina nodded.

Rosie shook her head in disbelief. "Do you know what could've happened to Dusty?"

"I know, and when I saw them compete today and how hard he tried for Hannah, I felt awful about what I had done and how I made fun of what he looks like."

Grandma handed her a tissue. "And what about when Baron got out? That wasn't Rosie and Carrie's fault either, was it?"

What? How did Grandma know that? Rosie wondered.

Katrina shook her head. "No. Actually, he never got out. I made the whole thing up."

Rosie's jaw dropped. "What? Why would you do that? Do you hate us?"

"No, I don't hate you. I wanted my dad to take Baron somewhere else, like to our old stable in Florida so I could be with my friends again."

Rosie slumped back against the seat. She didn't know what to think. They all sat in silence for a few moments. A street-light cast enough light through the truck window that she could see Katrina's face. The girl looked miserable.

"It's late, and we have a long drive," Grandma said. "We'll talk about this tomorrow." She started the truck and pulled into the line of vehicles headed for the exit.

Rosie moved as far to the left as possible so she wouldn't accidentally touch Katrina. She was so angry she felt as if she might explode. She crossed her arms and pressed them tightly against her body to help hold her feelings inside. It was going to be a long ride home.

Chapter 13

Sometimes Love is Blind

Rosie felt herself being jostled. She opened an eye and saw her grandmother sitting on one side of the bed and Carrie on the other.

Grandma squeezed Rosie's arm. "Are you awake?"

Rosie blinked. *What was going on? Had it all been a dream about Katrina letting Dusty out of the barn?* She rubbed her eyes and sat up. "I'm awake now, unless you two are in my dream."

Grandma shook her head. "No. It's not a dream. We need to talk about what happened with Katrina."

Rosie felt some of the anger from the previous night returning. She looked around. "Where is she?"

"When I peeked in the guest room, she was still asleep. Your mom and dad and I will talk to her after breakfast."

Rosie thought back over the past several weeks. "I don't understand it, Grandma."

"You mean why Katrina would do those things?"

"Any of it. You told us not to judge by outward appearances, and I was trying not to with Katrina. But right from the start I felt kind of nervous about her. I mean, none of the people I know look like that." Rosie looked at Carrie. Although her sister was silent, Rosie felt she was thinking some of the same things. They both turned to their grandmother.

Grandma shifted her position on the bed. "Remember Jacqui's great-great-grandfather, Wink?"

The girls nodded.

"Many people were quick to judge him based only on the color of his skin. That was unfair because that's the way God created him. They didn't take the time to see beyond skin color to what he was really like."

"But I've seen what Katrina is like. She's not very nice," Rosie said. "Just like I thought when I first saw her. She lied to get us in trouble, and Dusty could have gotten hurt when she let him out."

Grandma ran her hand through her hair. "Oh, my! This isn't quite as simple as I made it sound." She rested her hand on the top of her head for a moment, thinking. "While it's true we can't judge only on outward appearances, sometimes they do reveal a little about what someone is like."

Rosie felt even more confused now.

"I certainly don't want you to think you should never 'judge' based on what people look like. That can be dangerous," Grandma warned. "God gave us common sense, so we need to use it. You two know you shouldn't trust strangers, right?"

Rosie and Carrie nodded.

"Katrina's piercings and tattoo are not the same as a person's skin color," Grandma continued. "That's not the way God made her. The question is why she would choose to do those things to herself."

"She said she thought her tattoo was cool," Rosie said.

Grandma nodded. "I suppose that's a common reason. I think many times it's to rebel or to get attention or fit in with a particular crowd. My guess is it's a little of all those with Katrina."

Carrie frowned. "Her dad sure doesn't pay much attention to her."

"You're right," Grandma agreed. "Lately she's been with us more than with him. And apparently her mother isn't around at all. I've never heard Katrina mention her."

Rosie pulled her knees up and wrapped her arms around them. She still felt angry about the things Katrina had done. "What if she keeps doing stuff here? Maybe she'll let Scamper or Majestic or Charley out next!"

Grandma patted Rosie's leg. "You have a strong sense of right and wrong, Rosie—and that's a good thing—but don't ever forget there are two sides to God. His justice and His mercy."

Rosie remembered how miserable Katrina had looked the night before. Maybe she really was sorry for what she had done. "I guess I can give her another chance."

Grandma smiled. "Isn't that what Sonrise Stable is all about?"

The girls nodded.

"I'm going to go start breakfast. Why don't you two see if she's awake yet and invite her down to eat?"

Rosie got dressed, and the girls hurried down the hall to the guest room. Rosie knocked on the door, but no one answered. "Katrina," she called out. Still no answer. She opened the door and leaned in. The bed was made, and Katrina was gone.

Rosie jerked the door shut and grabbed Carrie's arm. "She ran away!"

Carrie looked skeptical. "Where would she go? The closest town is thirty miles away."

"She's probably riding Baron. That would be a lot faster than walking. Maybe she's heading to Florida!"

Carrie shook her arm loose. "Should we tell Grandma?"

"Let's look in the barn first." Rosie took off down the back stairs and out the door. She ran to the barn and opened the big sliding door on the boarders' side. Baron was in his stall, but she didn't see Katrina. She wasn't in the lounge either.

"Let's check the other side," Carrie said.

When they were halfway across the arena, Rosie saw someone in Scamper's stall. "Hey! Get out of there! What are you doing to my horse?"

She could feel the anger rising up inside her. "Come on, Carrie! I knew it! She's going to let Scamper out." Rosie ran to the gate, flung it open, and hurried through.

She skidded to a stop when she saw the wheelbarrow outside Scamper's stall. "Wha—?" She turned to Katrina. "What are you doing?"

Katrina emptied the pitchfork into the wheelbarrow. "What does it look like I'm doing? I'm cleaning his stall."

"B ... but ..." Rosie sputtered. "You're not supposed to do that."

Katrina looked down at the ground. "Hey, I'm sorry. I know I've been a jerk. It's just that things have been hard

..." She sniffed and wiped her nose on her sleeve. "Since my mom left."

Rosie looked from Katrina to Scamper and back. She remembered when she had learned that Billy's mother died when he was young. She felt the same sinking feeling in her stomach, and her anger began to evaporate. "It's okay."

Carrie nodded.

Katrina leaned back against the stall and petted Scamper. "Is your grandma going to kick Baron and me out?"

Rosie was surprised. Katrina had tried so hard to get her dad to take Baron somewhere else. Now she was worried about being kicked out of Sonrise Stable? "You mean you want to stay?"

Katrina nodded and smiled almost shyly. "Yeah."

"What about your friends?" Rosie asked.

"I guess they really aren't such good friends. I haven't heard from any of them for a while, and when I do they mostly just make fun of people."

Rosie raised her eyebrows.

"I know. I know. I've got that down pretty well myself." Katrina raked the shavings in the stall. "Do you think I'll be able to stay?"

"I'm pretty sure you will," Carrie said.

Rosie smiled. "You'll probably have to sit through one of Grandma's sermons first, though."

Katrina's eyes widened. "Your grandma's a preacher?"

Rosie laughed. "No. I'm just kidding, but she does like to preach. I'm sure she'll come up with a lesson for you from all this."

"I went to church a few times with my mom," Katrina said, "but that was a long time ago."

Rosie thought Katrina was going to cry. "You can go with us whenever you want."

"Okay. Maybe I will." Katrina went back to work on the stall.

Rosie grabbed a pitchfork off the wall. "You don't have to clean up after my horse."

"Yeah, he is the messiest horse in the barn," Carrie laughed.

"No, he isn ..." Rosie stepped into the stall and looked around. "Well ... maybe he is."

Scamper sniffed her pockets in search of a mint. "Sorry, boy. No more free treats for you." She pushed him away. "You have to earn them now. I'm going to teach you some tricks."

"What will you teach him first?" Katrina asked.

"If I can get Billy to build a pedestal, I'm going to teach Scamper to stand on it."

Carrie laughed. "You don't have to teach him that. He already tries to stand on everything—gates, fences, wheelbarrows." She turned to Katrina. "You should've seen him the day he stepped into the wheelbarrow."

Rosie glanced nervously at the stall door. "Yeah, don't keep that door open too wide or he may climb in it again."

Katrina closed the door a little more.

"At least Scamper didn't lay down with me in the creek, like Zach did," Rosie said.

"What?" Katrina said. "Your horse laid down in a creek?"

Carrie laughed and explained all about that adventure.

"You guys have so much fun together." Katrina bit her lip and brushed away a tear. "I wish I had a sister."

Rosie and Carrie turned toward each other, smiled, and nodded.

Katrina looked at them. "What?"

"You remember when I told you that Carrie and I were twins born two months apart?"

Katrina nodded.

"We could be triplets—with you born three years earlier," Rosie said.

Katrina smiled. "You mean it?"

Rosie and Carrie nodded.

"Yeah, I'd like that." Katrina looked down at the floor. "I'm really sorry for the way I've been acting. I guess I have a lot of apologizing to do—like to Billy and Hannah."

"Oh! Oh!" Rosie jumped up and down.

Carrie leaned into the stall. "What is it now?"

"I have the greatest idea!" Rosie opened the door and motioned for Katrina to follow her out.

Katrina stepped into the barn aisle. She and Carrie stood staring at Rosie.

"Our first project as triplets!" Rosie looked around to see whether there was anyone else in the barn. "We have to be quick before someone sees us."

"What are you talking about?" Carrie said.

Rosie leaned forward and whispered, "A trophy and ribbon for Dusty—his prize for winning the Extreme Cowboy Race!"

"But he didn't win," Carrie whispered back. She looked around. "Why are we whispering? There isn't anyone else out here."

"Okay." Rosie spoke in a normal voice. "Technically he didn't win, but he was the crowd favorite. That should count for something."

Katrina looked puzzled. "But we don't have a trophy or ribbon."

"Oh, yes we do." Rosie quickly explained to Katrina how Billy had cheated Scamper and her out of first place at the county fair the year before and how Billy had surprised her with the trophy and ribbon later as a peace offering. "Come on. Let's go get them!"

Rosie took off for the house with Carrie at her heels. When she was almost out of the barn, she looked back and saw Katrina still standing there. "Come on." Rosie waved to her.

Katrina hesitated, then ran to catch up with them.

"Oh, there you are," Grandma said as the girls raced through the front door. "I was getting worried about you. Are you ready for breakfast?"

"In a few minutes, Grandma." Rosie paused to catch her breath. "We have something really important to do."

Grandma waved the girls on. A herd of stampeding elephants couldn't have made much more noise than the three girls did running up the wooden stairs in their riding boots. A few minutes later they reappeared with the trophy, ribbon, a white poster board, and a few markers.

Grandma smiled as the girls rushed out the front door and back to the barn.

"I'll work on the poster while you two hang the trophy and ribbon on Dusty's stall." Rosie sat on the floor, popped the lid off a red marker, and began writing.

Carrie found a piece of baling twine and tied the trophy to the front of Dusty's stall.

"What about this?" Katrina held out the blue ribbon.

Carrie took it from her. "I'll tie it to the trophy."

"No, wait!" Rosie jumped up. They turned to look at her.

"Let's give it back to Billy."

Carrie shrugged. "It's okay with me."

Rosie looked at the sign Billy had tacked onto his mule's stall. "Sassy—Owned by William King." She took the marker and added a line below it. "Next Year's Extreme Cowboy Race Winner!" Then she drew a smiley face at the end.

Carrie looped the string from the ribbon around the tack that held the sign.

Rosie stood back and admired it. "Perfect!" She hoped the sign and ribbon would make Billy smile again. She returned to the poster. So far she had only written Dusty's name. "What should the poster say?"

"How about 'The Horse with Heart?'" Katrina suggested.

Carrie picked up one of the markers and tapped it on her chin. "Sometimes Love is Blind."

Rosie looked at her. "What does that mean?"

"Hannah loved Dusty so much that she didn't see how awful his eyes looked."

Rosie nodded. "That's good. Why don't we put them both on the poster?"

Underneath Dusty's name, Rosie wrote 'Extreme Cowboy Race Winner!' Then she handed the marker to Katrina so she could write her phrase. Carrie added hers next. They each signed the poster, and Rosie ran to get her hammer and a few tacks.

Carrie and Katrina held the poster up to the stall door. Rosie paused for a moment. The red handle of the hammer made her think of the red roan mare, then Charley, Wink, and Katrina. First Samuel 16:7—she didn't think she would ever forget that verse. She smiled and pounded a couple tacks into the poster.

"Someone's coming!" Carrie said.

Rosie ran to the front of the barn and peeked out the door. "It's Hannah and Dusty!" She raced back and herded Carrie and Katrina into the empty stall directly across from Dusty's.

Rosie hesitated a moment, then turned and walked back to Dusty's stall. She pulled the five-dollar bill out of her pocket and wedged it between the horse's legs on the top of the trophy. It wasn't close to the amount of money Hannah had hoped to win in the race, but it would help.

She crossed the aisle and slipped between Carrie and Katrina, sliding the door almost shut with just enough of an opening so they could all watch Hannah lead Dusty to his stall.

Rosie crouched down, waiting for the sound of hooves entering the barn. She was so excited she could hardly keep still. Sassy sensed that her friend was back. Rosie could hear her pacing back and forth. The mule called out to Dusty with her unique voice.

Rosie glanced briefly at Katrina and saw her smile. It made Rosie feel good. She realized that this girl who had appeared to be an enemy for so long was beginning to look like a friend.

Beka and Stormy

The fictional Hannah and her horse, Dusty, are based on Beka (Weaver) Setzer and her Appaloosa gelding. Stormy was in fact the first, and to my knowledge only, completely blind horse to ever compete in the Extreme Cowboy Race, a national event created by Craig Cameron.

When they participated in the 2010 race at Equine Affaire in Columbus, Ohio, Beka was twenty. Stormy was fourteen and had been blind for five years. Beka and Stormy were selected as one of the top thirty-six teams from across the country to compete in the race, based on the application video Beka submitted.

The pair finished twentieth, beating sixteen other teams. I was in the stands that day watching them—with tears running down my cheeks. It was the most inspiring horse performance I have ever seen.

Nationally recognized horse trainer, John Lyons, called Stormy "the Seabiscuit of our time."

Check the *Outward Appearances* book page on sonrisestable.com for links to Stormy's application and competition videos to see the real Beka and Stormy in action. You'll also find links to Stormy's Facebook page and other articles about the pair.

James Winkfield

"Sorry, you can't come in."

"But we—" The elderly man stared at the wood grain in the door that had just been slammed shut inches from his face. When the wave of humiliation faded, he turned to his daughter.

Her eyes flashed with anger. "They have to let us in. You're the guest of honor." She reached up to bang on the door, but he caught her hand. Taking a deep breath, he straightened his suit and knocked calmly.

The doorman frowned when he saw the woman and the short, thin man still standing at the entrance. "We don't allow you people to come in," he stated firmly and started to close the door again.

The small man gripped the edge of the door with surprising strength. "Wait! You don't understand. I have a special invitation."

The doorman paused.

"*Sports Illustrated*," the woman added. "They invited my father. He's a guest of honor at the banquet."

The doorman looked from the woman to the man. "Wait here." He closed the door in their faces again.

The man squeezed his daughter's hand and smiled at her, but her face remained stormy. Tantalizing odors drifted out from the hotel banquet room as they waited—split-pea soup, baked potato, and prime rib. After what seemed an eternity, the ornate wooden door that had shut them out opened again, and they were quietly ushered inside to a table by themselves.

That day, something stronger than a door separated them from the other guests. James Winkfield and his daughter, Liliane, were black.

It was May 1961, the Brown Hotel in Louisville, Kentucky. *Sports Illustrated* had recently written a feature article on Jimmy Winkfield (Wink). Winkfield, now in his eighties, was the last black jockey to win the Kentucky Derby, with back-to-back victories in 1901 and 1902.

Many people are not aware of the important role black jockeys played in the early days of horse racing. In the first Kentucky Derby, thirteen of the fifteen jockeys were black. Black riders won fifteen of the first twenty-eight Derbies. Little is known about many of those men. News reports at that time often gave the credit for wins to the owners of the horses or even to the horses themselves, rather than to the skillful jockeys who rode them.

As horse racing became more lucrative, whites began to vie for the jockey roles. The Jockey Club, formed in 1894, often denied licenses to blacks. The black jockeys who did race were subjected to violence by some of the white riders.

In a race, they might box in a horse and rider, bump or whip another jockey's horse, or slip their foot under the rider's stirrup and try to flip him out of the saddle. These techniques kept the black jockeys out of the winner's circle. Since owners hired jockeys based on their performance, the demand for black riders declined. Henry King finished tenth in the 1921 Derby. It would be seventy-nine years before another black jockey would ride in the race.

Although almost not allowed in the front door, Jimmy Winkfield shook off the insult and enjoyed the fine food at the banquet. He and jockey Roscoe Goose reminisced about the days when they used to compete against each other. Goose was the only white person to speak to Winkfield and his daughter that night.

Born in Chilesburg, Kentucky, in 1882, Wink was the youngest of eighteen children. He began racing at the age of fifteen. In addition to the two Derby victories, he won the Russian Derby four times, the Czar's Prize three times, the Russian Oaks five times, and the Warsaw Derby twice.

With 2,600 lifetime wins in the U.S. and internationally, Winkfield is considered one of the greatest jockeys of all time. He raced until he was almost fifty years old; then with his son, Robert, he devoted his time to training horses and jockeys at their stable in France.

Even as late as 1971, racial prejudice was evident when Marjorie Weber, a Kentucky journalist, visited the Winkfields and wrote:

> Mr. Winkfield is a gentle, dear, elderly little man. They all have so much culture and fineness that it is difficult to think that … you know what I am trying to say … they are colored or partly so. I mean nothing vicious about this at all … please, believe me.

In 2000, Marlon St. Julien became the first black jockey to ride in the Kentucky Derby since Henry King in 1921. St. Julien finished seventh out of nineteen riders. His appearance in the Derby attracted considerable media attention. In response to questions about his skin color, St. Julien stated, "I just want to be considered as one of the best riders in the country, whether black, white, purple, blue, or brown."

I think Wink would have agreed. Thirty years after his death in 1974, James Winkfield was inducted into the Hall of Fame of the National Museum of Racing.

Reference:
Wink: The Incredible Life and Epic Journey of Jimmy Winkfield by Ed Hotaling

Blind Horses

Many horses, like Beka Setzer's Stormy, can continue to be ridden and lead productive lives after going blind. Trainer, John Lyons, owned an Appaloosa, Bright Zip, who went completely blind in his twenties after an allergic reaction to medication. Lyons continued to use the blind horse for many years in his training seminars and clinics.

Too often, people assume that a blind horse can no longer lead a useful life but will at best serve as an expensive pasture ornament. They may be advised by a veterinarian to put the horse down, or other people may suggest that they get rid of the animal.

Sissy Burggraf, founder of Lost Acres Horse Rescue and Rehabilitation in Chillicothe, Ohio, has gained an appreciation for blind horses through her experience caring for these special animals for nineteen years. She shares some of her insights in the following interview.

How have you seen people respond when their horse goes blind?

Unfortunately, the general attitude of people toward blind horses is not good. I'm always puzzled when people are not willing to give these horses a chance. A blind dog or cat usually receives sympathy and compassion, but the first response to a horse becoming blind is too often to want to get rid of it. I've heard a variety of reasons.

The horse is dangerous because it can't see—
Well, any horse—blind or sighted—can be dangerous if you aren't careful.

The owners have young children, and they are afraid the blind horse will harm them—
Extreme caution should be used with children around any horse.

It's too expensive to keep them—
A blind horse doesn't cost any more to keep than a sighted one.

I want a horse that I can ride—
Many blind horses can continue to be ridden and may perform as well or better than a sighted horse.

You mean blind horses aren't dangerous?

As with people, losing sight is a frightening experience. Horses are potentially most dangerous while in the process of losing their sight. During this time they may only see shadows or partial objects. They spook more easily because they know something is out there, but they can't tell exactly what it is.

Horses that lose their sight will need time to adjust. Some do this rather quickly. While I wouldn't set it as an exact time, it's been my experience that most horses accept their blindness within three months. Rarely, a horse won't adjust at all. Thankfully, this is in very few cases, as the horse that cannot accept his loss of sight should be humanely euthanized. I have been fortunate that all of the horses at LAHRR have accepted their blindness.

How do you think horses figure out the layout of their environment?

My first experience with a blind horse was a big Morgan mare named Shadow. At the time, we didn't own our farm, so LAHRR rented facilities which meant the horses were stalled with daily turnout. I came into the barn one day and noticed a huge mound of sawdust in the middle of Shadow's stall. I cleaned her stall, straightening out the sawdust, making it nice and pretty for her, the way it should be—only to come in the next day and find that mound of sawdust in the middle of the stall again.

It took five days for this hardheaded human to realize the horse was doing this to make markers for herself. It was so many steps to her feed, so many to her water, her hay and her salt. She was a much happier horse when I just cleaned her stall and left the sawdust rearranging to her!

Now, when a blind horse first arrives at LAHRR, he is placed in a stall with an attached outside paddock. The horse is led to the water inside the stall, and I carefully splash a little onto his muzzle so he knows where to get a drink.

The horse is then led into the paddock and gently "bumped" into each of the panels, teaching him where the boundaries are. The horse has the freedom to go in and out of the stall at will and can get to know the blind horses in the adjoining pasture without actually being turned out with them yet.

After a day or two, when the horse seems comfortable with his surroundings, he is turned out with the other blind horses in the field.

What's different about handling a blind horse?

When you think about it, the only thing that makes blind horses different from sighted horses is the fact that they can't see! Sounds like a "duh!" statement, doesn't it? If your sighted horse was asleep when you entered the stall, the first thing you would do is speak to him so you wouldn't startle him. Then you would approach him. That's the same thing you do with a blind horse.

When working with sighted horses, you speak to them when approaching from behind to let them know it is you and not another horse or a predator. However, with blind horses, you speak to them when approaching from any direction to avoid frightening them. After speaking to them, if close enough, reach out and touch them. That's all there is to it.

Do I have to keep my blind horse in a stall to keep him safe?

At LAHRR, our blind horses are kept in a field with a run-in shelter. They come into the barn only to eat. To bring them in, I go to the gate, call to them to get their attention, and then clap my hands to give them the direction I want them to come. Once they get to the barn, I open the gate and they come in, on their own, and each goes into his own stall.

All of LAHRR's horses, not just the blind ones, come into the barn to eat. This prevents fighting between the horses and allows for their food intake to be monitored. Being off-feed is one of the first signs of illness in a horse.

When they've finished eating, I lead the blind horses back to the gate where they return to the pasture and usually head straight to the watering trough.

Horses often communicate with physical gestures, like flattening their ears or snaking their head at another horse. A blind horse will miss those signals, so it is important to make sure your horse is not turned out with a horse that will bully him.

All but one of our blind horses are kept in a field together. Visitors to LAHRR frequently can't believe the horses are blind. They live independently without the help of any kind of guide animal. There is a sighted horse in the field; however he is there for his own protection. The horses in the other fields pick on him.

What kind of fence is best for a blind horse?

As with people, when a horse loses his sight, the other senses become more highly developed. This enables them to hear, smell, and sense things that sighted horses do not. Board, vinyl, and field fencing may be used. High tensile fencing and barbed wire are not recommended for any horse, especially a blind one.

All of our fields are fenced in vinyl with electric braid running across the top. I use vinyl for the safety of the horses. They can't get their feet or legs caught in it, and because of its strength, they can't run through it.

Check your fields occasionally for holes that may appear from groundhogs or other animals. Watch for twines or wires from hay bales and any other objects that the horse may trip on or fall over. This should be done for sighted horses also.

What characteristics are required for the owner of a blind horse?

Patience is the major ingredient needed to care for blind horses. Until a blind horse fully trusts you, he may appear a little slower in his actions, hesitating to readily follow you or go to an unfamiliar place; but if you were blind, would you let a stranger lead you to someplace you didn't know?

Once that trust is earned, however, what a beautiful reward! Your horse will come to you when called, follow you as you walk, and what wonderful riding horses!

Can I really ride my blind horse?

Blindness doesn't affect horses' intelligence, their desire to please their owner, or their ability to be useful. If you rode your horse before, there is generally no reason why you can't continue to do so after he becomes blind. As with handling the horse on the ground, it's important to use your voice to communicate with him. Training your horse to respond to voice commands like "whoa" and "step up" can be helpful.

Once your trust is fully earned, you may find that your blind horse will go places and do things some sighted horse won't. Why? Because they can't see what the sighted horse fears—things like going through mud or water, over obstacles, and crossing bridges.

As your horse's confidence increases, you'll be able to enjoy the faster gaits—cantering or even a full-out gallop!

Given the chance, a blind horse can be a wonderful, faithful, companion and riding horse. They thrive on attention, love to be loved, and love to give love. They love life—they just can't see it.

Because LAHRR no longer adopts horses out, our turnover is very low and our facility often full. Although we can't always accept horses, we do work as a support outreach for people who own blind horses and need help or advice. If you have a question regarding blind horses, or any horse, please feel free to contact us. If we don't know the answer, we will find it for you!

Sissy Burggraf

www.lostacresrescue.org

The Sonrise Stable Series

Available at sonrisestable.com & amazon.com